C000147583

SPILLING THE BEANS

Lesley McCean

In support of

**The
ROYAL
MARSDEN
Cancer Charity**

SPILLING THE BEANS

...a day in the life of a coffee shop

SHORT STORIES BY JUST WRITE

Self-published by Just Write, Amersham

First published in Great Britain 2014

Collection ©Just Write 2014

Individual stories are the copyright of their authors, as follows:

Ristretto and *Double Espresso* ©Lesley Close

Macchiato, Iced Crush and *Chai Latte* ©Richard Hopgood

Hot Chocolate and *Peppermint Tea* ©Angela Haward

Café au Lait, Cappuccino and *Mocha* ©Liz Losty

Freddolatte and *Flat White* ©Linda Cohen

Black Americano, Hot Water and *Filter Coffee* ©Chris Payne

Iced Coffee and *Hazelnut Steamer* ©Debbie Hunter

Decaf Single Espresso ©Vicky Trelinska

A Cup of Tea ©Emma Dark

Instant Coffee ©Phil Tysoe

ISBN 9 780993 122200

Design and artwork by Oliver Payne and Stuart Tennant.

Printed and bound in Great Britain.

25% of the proceeds from the sale of each copy will be donated to the Royal Marsden Hospital (Registered Charity Number 1095197).

Just Write is RMCC supporter number 240434.

Introduction

This set of stories is the result of Sally Norton's decision to run creative writing classes (called Just Write) in Amersham. The authors were all members of that group when, at the end of term in June 2013, they decided they couldn't bear to wait until late September to meet and write again. Extra mural sessions were arranged, at the last of which someone said 'Wouldn't it be fun to work together and write a set of stories?' and someone else added 'They could all take place on the same day in a coffee shop…' and the rest is history. Sally agreed to write an introduction after reading all the stories.

***

Fiction writing is often thought to be a lonely art form. The book you have in your hand disproves this theory. This wonderful collection of short stories is written by a group of writers who originally met in my creative writing class in Amersham, and it is as clever, funny and sensitive as the people who created it.

As well as working individually to write their own unique short stories, the writers have also worked together in an incredibly disciplined way to set them all in the same coffee shop on the same day. This means you, the reader, can dip in and enjoy a single story or, better still, read them all as a whole.

There is so much new writing talent here, as you'll soon discover. You'll find fascinating, complex characters, clever twists and some really beautiful writing. There's also been a huge amount of skill and behind-the-scenes work done in editing, designing and producing this book so well.

I'm so proud of the whole team who came together to create this book. I wish I could take some credit for it but I can't – I just made the tea and passed around the biscuits.

I hope you enjoy reading *Spilling the Beans* as much as I have.

Sally Norton

DAVID'S STORY

Hi. My name is David, I'm 23 years old and in July 2014 I was diagnosed with a rare form of bone cancer called Ewing's Sarcoma. Though it was difficult to identify at first, as soon as it was confirmed I began treatment at the Royal Marsden Hospital in Sutton. I am currently half way through nine cycles of chemotherapy and will undergo radiotherapy, more chemotherapy and possibly surgery afterwards. Though the treatment is aggressive, it is working! Already the main tumour has shrunk to less than half its original size and the smaller secondaries have disappeared altogether. I never expected such drastic improvements in my condition in such a short amount of time. I am so very grateful for the high quality of care I have experienced here and the trouble taken to keep me, my partner and my family informed of any progress and changes.

Although there is some NHS funding, much of my treatment is funded by the Royal Marsden Cancer Charity and they really need more money to continue providing and improving the different treatments which are saving lives — including mine! So please, if you can, buy this book and help this incredible cause. Thank you.

DEDICATION

Dedicated to The Royal Marsden Hospital, for the wonderful work they do.

In support of

The ROYAL MARSDEN Cancer Charity

About The Royal Marsden Cancer Charity

Every year The Royal Marsden provides treatment and care for more than 50,000 cancer patients and is at the forefront of cancer research. Its work influences how all cancer patients are treated and cared for, not just in its own hospitals but all over the world.

With the help of The Royal Marsden Cancer Charity, The Royal Marsden can continue to push the boundaries and benefit cancer patients, wherever they are.

The Royal Marsden Cancer Charity raises money to help The Royal Marsden provide world-class diagnosis, treatment and care for cancer patients, and supports the hospital's pioneering work in cancer research.

By supporting The Royal Marsden in this way the charity aims to make life better for people with cancer everywhere and strive for a future without it.

Acknowledgements

Debbie Hunter, Angela Haward and Lesley Close edited the texts and they would like to acknowledge their gratitude to Sally Norton, Richard Hopgood and Chris Payne who helped with that process.

Stuart Tennant managed both the creative and production aspects of this book. He worked on the initial concepts with help from JoJo Blythen, and with Oliver Payne who provided the design, typography and artwork. The illustrations were provided by Juliette Orton and Chas Burton.

Above all, the editors would like to thank the authors who wrote the stories, Janet Mears for her superb proofreading (any remaining mistakes are the fault of the editors, not Janet), and the many anonymous 'test' readers whose input improved the stories immensely.

CONTENTS

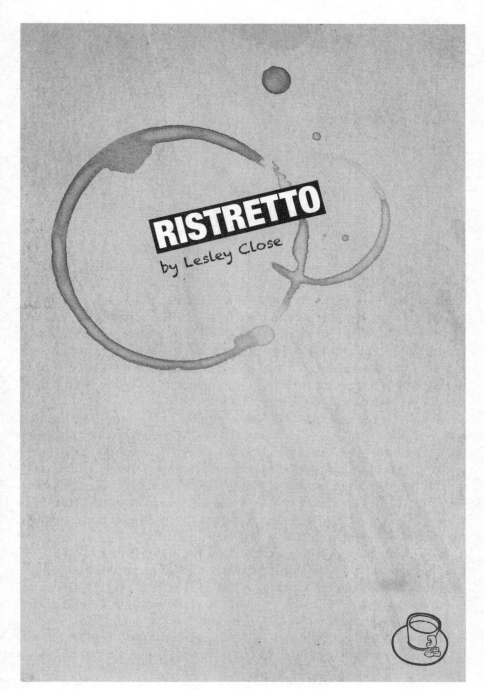

RISTRETTO

by Lesley Close

I T was raining gently when Antonia arrived for work that Tuesday morning in October. She looked at her watch – good, still a few minutes to go until five, plenty of time for a fag. She smoked as slowly as possible, the curling smoke mingling with the misty rain. Antonia loved her job but she sometimes wished she could start work a bit later. It would be different if she allowed herself to bake the morning goods the previous afternoon, but she was a perfectionist who suffered for her art. Stale croissants and dry pain au chocolat wouldn't sell – they needed to be freshly baked every day.

Her first cigarette butt of the day went into the fire-proof pouch her partner Jackie had given her when Darren banned smoking in the car park. Emblazoned with a skull and crossbones, it was another attempt to put Antonia off smoking: every time she acted responsibly and binned her butts rather than stamping them out underfoot, she faced Jackie's reminder of her mortality. But Antonia was made of strong stuff and it would take more than a piratical picture to put her off a habit which provided her with comfort and sustenance.

Unlocking the door, she switched on the lights and smiled at the simplicity of the code she tapped to turn off the alarm. What was there to pinch? Only Darren's precious coffee machine and his array of expensive syrups. She could see them now, just beyond the end of the corridor and gently illuminated by its light.

Before doing anything else, Antonia put her hand round the door into the counter area to turn on the coffee machine. Despite the first

14

hit of nicotine, she needed a shot of caffeine in the morning. She drank ristretto, the tiniest measure of water the machine could use to make a coffee. Thick and dark, it gave her just the right amount of energy to start baking.

While waiting for the machine to warm up she switched on the lights in the kitchen, turning her head away and closing her eyes against the sudden flashing glare of the fluorescent tubes. She had loved baking last summer in southern Italy, where dawn and her shift started at the same time. No need for lights there, but no real money either in the cooperative. Still, it had been fun and she wouldn't have met Jackie otherwise.

In the staffroom she hung up her coat and opened her locker, taking out a set of clean whites. She enjoyed wearing a uniform, even an unbranded one like this: it made her feel that she belonged in a place. She'd worn her own clothes to work in the Italian sunshine, and it hadn't felt like a proper job. But that was the whole point, she supposed: a bunch of fellow soul-searchers living in the sun and earning money from tourists.

Back at the now-awake coffee machine, she downed a ristretto in one then made another to take with her to the kitchen. After putting the tiny coffee cup on a shelf and turning on the radio – classical music, although Darren would re-tune it to Radio Two when he arrived – Antonia washed her hands. She turned to the bowl of sourdough on which nature had worked its reliable magic over the last three days. She gently pressed the slightly-glistening surface of the dough, admiring the silky-soft kneading-ready texture and greeting it like a warm friend. 'An excellent start to the day,' she thought as she replaced the cover. She would start another batch before she left work this afternoon and check the other ongoing batch.

She opened the fridge and took out a block of fresh yeast. Cutting off a chunk, she crumbled it into a mixing bowl on the scales until the quantity was exactly right. Adding a spoonful of water, she mixed it to a smooth opaque cream before leaving it for the few moments it would take to gather the other ingredients.

This was the part of her job that she loved best, mixing some of the yeasty liquid with water then adding it to the flour and kneading the dough. She loved stretching and turning the ball in her hands, and was secretly thrilled every time she removed the risen dough from the prover and saw that it had doubled in size.

When the dough had started its ninety-minute proving Antonia turned to the sourdough which, made into ciabatta loaves, sliced and filled with salad leaves or roasted vegetables and hummus, was so popular with Darren's yummy mummy clients.

But now it was time for the first clean up of the day. Antonia snapped rubber gloves over her hands and filled a bucket with hot water. She used a disposable cloth for the stainless steel work surfaces, sweeping the water onto the floor before washing and mopping it. Within ten minutes the kitchen was clean again.

Antonia peeled off the gloves, washed her hands and turned her attention to shaping dough into bread rolls ready for proving. The rich croissant dough was ready and, as she wrapped pieces of plain chocolate inside some of it, she thought about what Jackie had said last night. She hadn't expected it: neither of them had ever mentioned starting a family. They'd talked about the future, but their plans had focused on opening their own café on the coast. They'd imagined making the most of the summer tourist trade so they could travel in the winter. At least, that had been their plan until last night . . .

Antonia shook her head to rid herself of distracting thoughts. Today's batch of baked goods was coming together nicely and it was getting on for seven – Beryl might come in early and the girls would definitely be here soon. Time for a break. Antonia picked up her cigarettes and headed for the back yard. The drizzle had eased – good: Beryl hated having to mop the floor all day to soak up umbrella and coat drips, and the mess some people brought in on their wet shoes was incredible. She lit up and leaned against the wall. Jackie had told her she'd have to stop smoking altogether if they decided to try for a baby. The thought of that made Antonia inhale even more deeply than usual and she sighed as she blew the smoke up into the lightening sky. She found the prospect of motherhood both exciting and terrifying at the same time. How would she and Jackie divide the labour? Hah – that was one heck of a Freudian slip! Jackie wanted to do the hardest part, but what role would Antonia play after the child was born? She would have to carry on earning to support them both – or rather the three of them. Could they still move away and make a go of it? That was an even more exciting and far less terrifying prospect than bringing a child into the world.

She and Jackie would have to talk again, tonight and on many nights to come, before they came to a final decision. Even then nothing was certain – Jackie's biological clock may already have stopped . . . And would they find a man who was willing to be a father, biological or practical or both, to their child?

Sighing again, Antonia heard Elizaveta and Maria before she saw them, their bubbly voices carrying across the yard as they arrived for work.

"Morning," she called, the first word she had spoken all day. She had whispered Goodbye to Jackie as she left their bedroom.

"'Ello," the girls said, almost in unison, as they made their way through the door into the coffee shop, turning on lights and bringing the place to life.

**

"Hi Antonia! Is this a good time?" Antonia looked up from mopping the kitchen floor again to see Darren leaving a trail of footprints on the wet tiles.

"Is it that time already?" she replied. The daily 'team meeting', as Darren insisted on calling it, took place at around ten-thirty, after the breakfast rush left and before the lunch crowd arrived. Antonia was proud of her work and looked forward to finding out how the previous day's baking had sold and discussing whether any changes were needed to their plan for the next few days. "Great! I could do with another coffee."

"In that case, madam, I am the answer to a maiden's prayer. I've brought a ristretto with me." Darren looked around for somewhere to put the cup then dragged a pair of stools out from under the work surface. He knew full well that she nearly always drank a ristretto while they talked, but that didn't stop him making out he was really thoughtful.

Sitting on the stool opposite Antonia, Darren smiled. "The croissants went down a storm today – that old guy had a ham and cheese one, as usual. There are hardly any left now, which says a lot. Thanks."

Thanks? Antonia was incredulous: Darren was *thanking* her? He must have had a compliment from a customer. Despite her mixed feelings about Darren, it was good to know the morning goods she baked every day were appreciated.

"So, any change for the menu for tomorrow?" she asked, wondering if she would get one of Darren's attempts at a joke for an answer.

Instead he said, "Something smells good." Antonia sniffed: she was immune to the routine, yeasty odours of her work. It was when she made special mixtures that she noticed them: cinnamon buns, herb loaves, nutmeg-scented egg custard tarts, pain au chocolat, cheese and onion rolls. She and Darren had worked out a set of menus which lasted ten days. Customers who came in once a week kept coming back to check out the specials, thinking that every day really was different.

Getting to the position they were in now, with many different items made fresh daily, had been a struggle. Darren had employed Antonia because of her baking skills but he had expected her to work with pre-prepared items. When this came up at her interview, over a cup of coffee while the shop was quiet, she had put her foot down and insisted that, if he wanted the coffee shop to be a real success, he should try her from-scratch methods for the first three months. He had reluctantly agreed – the kitchen had not been equipped to cope with those methods and the company had had to spend some money to bring it up to anything like Antonia's specification. But, so far, she was winning and the customers enjoyed her ciabattas and baguettes as well as the light wholemeal and crusty white rolls she made to be filled and the soda bread which went so brilliantly with soup. And every day she made at least one sweet item, mostly for her own enjoyment.

With this being half-term week, Antonia and Darren had agreed to offer more child-friendly food than usual. She had suggested cupcakes but Darren was adamant that the yummy mummies would not want their children to be hyped-up with sugar. So, for today's offering, Antonia had made crumpets and fruit breads. It was asking a lot of any single-handed baker's skills to make several different types of bread every day but at least the quantities were small.

Antonia was determined to show that she could do everything that was asked of her. "That delicious smell is the fruit bread I made earlier for the kids," she answered. "Do you want a slice with your coffee?"

"No thanks," Darren drawled. "Not right now. And there are no changes to the menu for tomorrow. I reckon we stick to the plan, what with it being half-term. Bloomin' kids – still, you've got to love 'em at the end of the day." He sighed, and picked up his mug.

Hearing Darren say the words 'love' and 'kids' reminded her of what Jackie had said last night and, for a moment, she stopped listening to him. The age gap between her and Jackie seemed to have widened overnight. Jackie's biological clock, ten years ahead of Antonia's, appeared to have started sending out alarm signals. That was the only reason she could think of for Jackie's out-of-the-blue announcement that she wanted to have a child. Her question "Who would make the best sperm donor?" was still reverberating around Antonia's mind.

How the heck should she know? They had plenty of gay friends who would probably help out, but Jackie said she wanted someone who would be involved with the baby forever. Most of the potential donors they knew were unlikely to want to change nappies, in Antonia's opinion. The ideal donor would be someone who already had a kid so you could be sure they actually *liked* them, but most of the fathers they knew were married and would not want to have a child outside their families.

"So that's the menus sorted, then." Darren's voice cut through her thoughts, and she looked up to see the day's delivery of flour arriving. Their meetings were often interrupted by the arrival of the van and the usual driver was happy to let Antonia do the carrying while he had a drink with Darren. Antonia was strong, slinging the sacks over her shoulder as though they were unruly children as she walked briskly from the van in the yard to the store room. Today a new driver, keen to make a good impression, grinned broadly at Antonia, winked lewdly at Darren, and carried the sacks himself. Alleluia! A man who didn't see Antonia as an Amazon. It was her own fault, she supposed: she was tall but not exactly slim and expressed herself in a forthright manner. But she was all-woman, as Jackie liked to remind her.

Taking advantage of the new guy's willingness to help and Darren's involvement with showing him the ropes, Antonia stepped outside for a smoke break. As she left, she heard the driver say, "She's gorgeous!"

Darren chuckled his response. "Don't bother, mate. You've got no chance with her."

Antonia stood under the overhanging roof and lit up, taking tiny sips of her cold but still drinkable ristretto between drags. Bliss! The van driver came out and said "Goodbye" in a different tone of voice, a curious look on his face. As he drove away, Antonia wondered how you go about asking someone to donate their sperm. She'd have to know someone really well before she'd feel anything less than blushingly, stammeringly awkward about asking.

Walking back to the kitchen, Antonia saw Darren coming out of the staff room. "I meant to tell you," he said. "I've been thinking about the specials for Christmas. We should talk about that at tomorrow's team meeting."

"I've been thinking about it too, and I've already got some ideas," Antonia replied. "We could have gingerbread people – not just men! – and stained glass window biscuits and *stollen* and *Pan de Pascua* from Chile and *Bolo-Rei Escangalhado* from Portugal and – "

"Hey!" interrupted Darren. "That's enough to feed the whole town! It's great that you're so enthusiastic about the idea. I love Christmas, I always have, and I love the idea of representing lots of different countries on the menu. The kids – and their parents – will love it! Thanks, Antonia." Darren grinned and walked back to the customers.

Antonia found herself wondering whether Darren would make a good sperm donor. He might be a bit mean sometimes, but his attitude towards her baking, his customers, the children who came into the coffee shop and, especially, his father showed that he had a kind heart. He had that salacious interest in lesbians common amongst straight men but he could forget about threesomes – or even 'normal' sex with Jackie. If he could be persuaded to provide what was needed for the turkey baster (or whatever people use these days – Antonia had no idea!) then maybe . . . ? But would he be willing to do it? And how would she ask him? That was a subject to be raised at a quite different type of 'team meeting'.

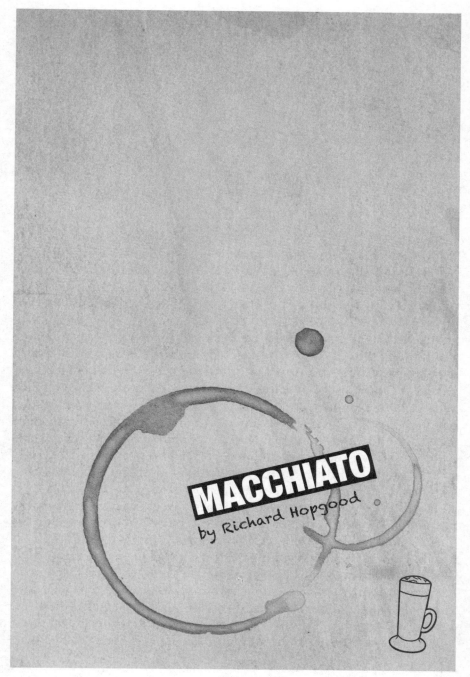

MACCHIATO

by Richard Hopgood

THE air had an autumnal chill as he strode in his robust leather brogues along the pavement towards the coffee shop. He sniffed the air appreciatively. The smell of damp leaves, ripe fruit, wood smoke and bare earth had the complexity of a good wine. All sorts of different notes, he reflected.

Arnold was in his sixties, a bachelor. He had trained as a lawyer at a London Inn of Court and worked, for a while, as a solicitor at a commercial firm in the West End, until the pressure had become too much for him. Most of his career had been spent at the Probate office of the Inland Revenue, where his knowledge of the law and meticulous attention to detail were well suited. Accuracy mattered more than speed, and he was not one to be hurried. Some of his most unpleasant memories were of being asked to meet ridiculous deadlines. He wrote, as he thought, slowly and deliberately: his long hand was elaborate, with graceful loops and a metronomic consistency.

He visited the coffee shop three times a week, unless he was away or ill. After the heart attack which had forced his early retirement, his doctor had told him to cut back on the alcohol and give up his pipe. So he had gradually stopped visiting the local, where he was accustomed to sit with a pint of brown, a bag of nuts and an ash tray on which to knock his pipe, listening to the blokey banter and telling the odd anecdote to people he had known and half-liked for years. The coffee shop was a good replacement. On his numerous trips to France with the local *Alliance Française*, he had always admired French café life, with its casual, understated style. There was none of the beery jocularity of the English pub or the fussiness of the English tea room. You could be as sociable or as private as you wished, and have whatever you wanted. It just was.

When he had first come up with the idea of swapping the local for the coffee shop, he had decided to sample three or four before making his choice. He did nothing without planning. So for two weeks he had appeared in different cafés, in his heavy brown duffle coat with his rucksack and Harrods' bag containing maps, books, his medication and several pairs of glasses. The first had been discounted because the Polish girl behind the counter had insisted he give his Christian name when he gave his order. He had been mortified when a bumptious young man had called out "Arnie!" when his coffee was ready. The second was also not favoured because the young blonde girl (Czech, he thought) insisted on getting him to sign up for a loyalty card despite his protestations that he was 'just trying things out'.

"You can have your fifth coffee for free – on the house," she cajoled.

"But I may never come here again . . . "

"But why would you not? Our coffee is *absolutely* the best!" she said, flashing an enthusiastic smile. He beat a hasty retreat.

The other two, local branches of global chains, had served his coffee in an enormous china mug which made him feel oddly childlike, as if he had entered a world of giants. The rather manic cheerfulness came across as sociability on speed. He half expected to be hugged at any moment, or surrounded by a choir of baristas singing him a special coffee song on his birthday. He found himself silently mouthing obscenities and chuckling at his own profanities. It would make a good addition to his store of anecdotes about himself.

The last coffee shop was not part of a chain, had *optional* loyalty cards, served tea and coffee in perfectly normal cups and had corners with proper tables and chairs, where the more reticent could linger, as well as low sofas and coffee tables for youngsters and children. Two of the staff were East European – from somewhere Baltic, he thought, as their language was not at all Slavonic. There was also a middle-aged woman who cleared the tables, a fresh-faced young man in a cheap grey suit whom he presumed was the manager and, in the kitchen, a tall woman dressed in a white uniform who apparently baked all the bread. That probably wasn't true, at least entirely, but the air was filled with the delicate floury fragrance of baking.

He had now been coming to the coffee shop for three years, knew the names of all the members of staff (not difficult because most wore badges) and had managed not to divulge his own name, although he was greeted with a smile of familiarity and even asked whether he wanted 'the usual'.

Today was, in fact, his birthday. He was sixty-seven. Not exactly a milestone, or at least not one he was aware of, although measured from the end of life no doubt there were all sorts of hidden milestones. But he thought he still had some years left to enjoy and, in his sunnier moments, he reflected that old age suited him. Nobody fussed about what would become of him or how he could change his ways for the better. He had become what he was and people finally accepted him. Sold as found. Take it or leave it. His eccentricities – the heavy duffle coat, as if he was always expecting a chill 1950s fog to steal over him, the bags, the planning, the love of routine and the terror of the unfamiliar – were all now lovable rather than odd. He noticed that, as they aged, some of his friends now 'hung loose', as his nephew would put it; they dropped the pretence of what they were not and ceased to hide their own little peculiarities. That made his own seem less extreme, more normal even.

He entered the coffee shop and dumped his bags by a corner table. "I'll look after them, darling, until you've given your order," said Beryl, the middle-aged table cleaner. She was bustling around clearing dirty cups and giving the glass table tops a quick spray and wipe. Arnold nodded, and wondered whether to tell her it was his birthday. Maybe later. At the counter Elizaveta, the shorter of the Baltic girls, put down her phone and smiled professionally at him.

"You like usual, sir? Cappuccino and cheese and ham croissant?" Arnold looked at the blackboard behind her. He felt like something different, a little treat to acknowledge that this was a different day.

"It's my birthday. I think I should try something different, don't you?"

"Your birthday? I wish you very happy day!" She shouted something to her Baltic compatriot, Maria, a taller blonde girl with a Nordic calm, who left the giant coffee machine she tended and came over.

"Very many happy returns," said Maria with a look of triumph, proud to have recalled this authentic English phrase.

"Why thank you," Arnold responded, with a flicker of a smile.

"How old you are?"

"How old am I?" replied Arnold, emphasising the correct word order. "Too old, I think. Sixty-seven."

"No!" they chorused together, with a look of theatrical astonishment. "You look so young!"

Now he knew they were lying, even having a joke at his expense. Nobody had ever accused him of looking younger than his years – indeed, for most of his life, people had consistently assumed he was older than he really was. "Well, thank you, but you don't have to pretend. I am sixty-seven, I look sixty-seven . . . And I feel sixty-seven . . . " A wave of melancholy stole over him. Maybe sixty-seven really was getting on. Almost seventy. The wrong side of sixty-five. Middle age was now the dark side of the moon. He felt old.

"We give you free coffee on the house, just for today, for your birthday. Perhaps you tell us your name now so we can sing Happy Birthday?"

"That won't be necessary," he said firmly, "but I'll take you up on the free coffee."

He scanned the board again and opted for a macchiato. He had no idea what it was but he liked the word. There was something stylish about it. Hell, he would give it a try. But he stuck to his cheese and ham croissant, having pondered and then rejected some more exotic alternatives.

The Baltic women were now talking rapidly to each other and laughing, He hoped it was not at his expense. He settled down at his table and delved into his Harrods' bag for his *Daily Telegraph* to read the obituaries and to check whether any new names had appeared on the list of people who shared his birthday. The latter was a disappointment. It was not a very illustrious list and the new names meant absolutely nothing to him, presumably young people whose fame and earning power were sufficient for even the *Telegraph* to notice them.

But the obituaries cheered him. A former QC and judge whom he knew by sight from countless dinners at Gray's Inn had died at the age of seventy-three. He had once spoken to Arnold, mistaking him for a barrister; Arnold had stuttered and blushed. "Don't worry, old chap," the now dead man had said. Kindly meant, no doubt, although Arnold resented being treated like a harmless old buffer. But now he was alive, and enjoying a free coffee on a crisp autumn day while he bit a chunk out of his croissant, and Sir Cedric Evans QC was dead. Better a live buffer than a dead . . . He searched for a word which would wittily dismiss the dead man, but lapsed into silence. *Dead Ced* . . . Mmm, not terribly good. It sounded like an anagram.

He came out of his reverie and looked around. Two young mothers in long coats and knee-length boots had come in with pushchairs and their two toddlers were climbing all over a leather sofa, squirming along the top and falling in a tangled heap behind it before repeating the circuit as if on an assault course. The mothers unbuttoned their coats and examined their phones before one of them rose to go to the counter. At another table, an elderly woman with immaculately coiffured white hair and rheumy eyes was bent over a large iced Danish pastry, which she was cutting into small pieces. She gulped her tea, looked around her, then ate the pieces with indelicate rapidity as if they might otherwise be stolen by the marauding small boys, who were now crawling after each other between the tables. She was probably right. He felt irritated with the young mothers for their insouciance, but would not have dreamed of saying anything.

He sipped his macchiato. It had quite a kick to it. He felt the bitterness of the espresso intensify on the back of his tongue before the milk froth spread a brief soothing balm. A sharp twinge in a rear molar reminded him that he needed to ring up his dentist. He had been ignoring the pain for a week now, but it was beginning to intrude. "Damn," he muttered.

Over by the young mothers there was a squawk and then a howling. One of the little boys had bumped his head against a chair leg. The other little boy stopped and looked in fascination as the tears rolled down his friend's face and the howls became louder. There was a kind of exasperation in his sobbing, Arnold thought, as it rose in a crescendo. Maybe he was cross with his mother, who looked down at him then resumed a conversation on her mobile.

"Oh my dear!" Beryl exclaimed as she bustled over with a cloth in one hand and a biscuit in the other. "What have you done, little fellow?"

She hauled the little boy to his feet and stroked his head with her hand.

"He's ok, he's always bumping into things," his mother shouted. "I think it's his age." She clamped her mobile to her ear again. "Yes, darling, Toby's bumped his head on something. No, it's all right, he's ok . . . "

Beryl's attention seemed to soothe the little boy, and he lapsed into quiet contentment when she gave him a chocolate chip cookie. "Here you are darling, this'll make you feel better. And here's one for you too, Charlie," she added, proffering one to the other little boy who had resumed crawling between the tables and was heading for Arnold. He paused to take the biscuit then continued his journey until he reached Arnold's legs, sensibly clad in thick cavalry twill trousers. Putting his hands on Arnold's knee caps, he hauled himself to his feet, took a bite of his biscuit, and offered the rest of it to Arnold.

"I think he likes you!" Beryl said, raising her eyebrows and grinning theatrically.

"Hello, little chap. What's that you've got in your hand?" Arnold asked. The boy looked at Arnold then fixated on his duffle coat toggles, one of which he began to twist to and fro whilst resting his other hand on Arnold's leg. "It's a duffle coat," Arnold said. "Only old fossils like me wear them nowadays." He chuckled at his own joke. "Careful you don't twist it too hard . . . "

"He's a little sweetie, isn't he?" Beryl remarked. Arnold didn't know whether she was referring to him or the child.

"Yes, he's a good little – "

"Here, Charlie, leave that man alone!" his mother interjected, with a rather unpleasant sharpness. "Come back here!"

Charlie looked at Arnold, then at his mother, and sat down as if he needed time to think. The woman rose from her chair, and yanked Charlie back by his arm. He started to yowl, but quickly quietened down when she pushed another biscuit towards him.

"I don't think that was necessary," Beryl murmured to Arnold as she cleared his cup and plate, and wiped the table. "Would you like something else, dear?"

Arnold felt irresolute. He had been really rather enjoying himself and, although he felt awkward with children, he was oddly touched when the little boy came over. Now he felt branded as somebody odd and vaguely unsafe. The more timid side of him felt he should leave the field to the young mothers to avoid further embarrassment. His stronger half felt this would be to concede ground unnecessarily. He had done nothing wrong – Beryl herself had as much as said so.

"Er, I think I'll have another coffee – and a glass of water please. Tap water will do."

Beryl bustled away. He felt pleased he had not given in. He resented the young mother's behaviour. 'Not a good mother,' he thought. 'Both suspicious and negligent.' He thought of his own mother, who had suffered a nervous breakdown after he was born. His sister had cared for him more than his mother so they had never really bonded. Even in old age, long after his domineering father had died, there was a coolness between them. His mother sometimes tried to show affection but it felt somehow false and inauthentic, a show for good form's sake. He never called her 'Ma' as his siblings did, only 'Mother'. The unhappiness of his childhood stole over him. Damn the woman, why did he have to think about her on his birthday? The thought spread across his mind like a drop of black ink in a pool of water.

The coffee arrived, and a small cake with a single candle on it, burning with a tiny wavering flame. "Here you are dear. Happy Birthday!" He looked up and Beryl was standing there with the two Baltic girls. Elizaveta bent down and kissed him on top of his head.

"Happy sixty-seven," they exclaimed together.

He felt alarmed, then surprised, and his face prickled with embarrassment before, to his consternation, his eyes filled with tears. He tried to smile jocularly, rose awkwardly to his feet, and deposited a kiss on Elizaveta's startled face before slumping back into his chair, accidentally dousing the candle's flame with his cuff.

"That's quite enough now . . . "

HOT CHOCOLATE

by Angela Haward

ANDREA knows it won't work. There isn't a parking space in sight. Maybe they could come back tomorrow. A little shudder of hope ripples somewhere in her midriff. She watches the shops slide past the window as Mum crawls up the High Street and right round the mini roundabout to come back in case someone's going. They aren't. The whisper in her head echoes once again – don't think about it.

"I'll have to stop on the double yellows, love, but I won't be able to come to the door with you. I'll watch you, though. You can do this. You walked to the car without holding my arm – and it's only a few yards to the coffee shop – look."

"Can't we do it tomorrow?" She doesn't think she's actually going to say it, but it slips out.

"You know we can't, love. Your appointment's at ten-thirty tomorrow. Look, I'll just sit here for a moment until you get inside – and I'll be back at eleven. I'll be right here – OK?"

Andrea's stomach clenches. She can't let them down. She forces herself to grip the door handle and notices how cold it feels under the damp heat of her palm. Don't think about it. Counting, just as they'd practised, she puts one foot, then the other on the pavement, lifts her head and breathes the diesel-tinged air. 1, 2, 3, 4 . . . The buildings, the sky, the traffic, the people – they lap round the edges of her mind, trying to breach the dam she's built there. 5, 6, 7, 8, 9 . . . Five more steps and she's touching the glass . . . 10, 11, 12 . . . She's in. She just catches the sound of Mum's car pulling away and merging with the morning traffic.

Her senses are unused to being assaulted simultaneously by scents, sounds and movement. After all, it's been two whole years. A wave of warm air carries the aroma of coffee with undercurrents of baking. The clatter of crockery conflicts with the whirr of the coffee machine and the chatter of voices from behind the counter. The therapist got it wrong. She should have asked Mum to come with her the first time. Don't think about it. 13, 14, 15 . . .

"Yes, can I help you?" One of the girls behind the counter is looking straight at Andrea questioningly. Andrea looks back at her, trying to remember what she should do.

"What would you like?" The girl tries again, glancing behind her customer as if to indicate that she is holding up the queue. But Andrea is the only one there.

"Ummm – hot chocolate." That's not it – she's not supposed to have that. But she'd said it now. It would have to do.

"Is that with whipped cream and a flake?"

Too many questions. They haven't gone through this at all. "Er – yes, yes, whatever." Don't think about it. Andrea knows she must be sounding a bit abrupt, but at least she's managed to say something. She stores up the small victory to report back at the appointment tomorrow.

"£2.99 please."

Andrea gives her three pound coins and receives her penny change – no receipt. But there has to be a receipt. That's part of the deal. A receipt with the date and time and what she has bought. She's got to show it tomorrow to prove that she managed to 'jump the first hurdle' (not her words). She screws up her courage.

"Umm – could I – could I have a receipt, please . . . ?" The girl looks vaguely surprised and examines the paper chain hanging from the till to identify the last one, before handing it to Andrea with an unintelligible grunt. She's forgotten a tray. The chocolate is almost too hot to hold.

Next challenge – where to sit. It would be easier if there was less choice. It's too early for the yummy mummies – she knew the therapist chose this time specifically to break her client in gently. Andrea avoids the old man gazing intently at the screen of his laptop – he may be old, but he's still a man – and settles on a table for two in the back corner so she can have her back and left arm against a wall.

The chocolate is thick and sweet as it seeps onto her tongue through the cold layer of cream. It reminds her of childhood bedtimes – warm and comforting like her fluffy winter pyjamas – the right choice. Another tick in the progress box for tomorrow.

The flake crumbles in her mouth like fairy dust and she's back for a moment in the sweet shop that isn't there any more, counting her pocket money to see if she has enough to buy another one. Her eyes close to savour the memory, so she hears, rather than sees, a person sit down at the table to her right. The clatter of a tray and the rustle of a coat being shed disturb her brief reverie.

She doesn't look – but her peripheral vision takes in a man – no more – just a man. Oh – God. She was told this might happen. They've practised. 11, 12, 13 – no, she's done 11. She's forgotten where she was. It isn't working. Don't think about it. But she is thinking about it. Her stomach clenches again. It's going to happen. She gasps – too late.

Her heart begins pounding out of her chest. Her throat closes and rapid breaths squeeze through the tiny gap in a loud wheeze. Tears ooze from her clenched eyelids as she waits for the next gasp. The urge to run is overpowering.

As she struggles to stand up, she feels a firm hand on her shoulder, pushing her back down. A male voice speaks quietly, gently, but with an inescapable air of authority.

"It's OK. It's just a panic attack. No-one's looking. Sit down and breathe into this bag – here."

He's holding a paper bag towards her face, already formed into a balloon shape and ready for use. He's been to The Card Shop – how does she manage to notice that? Don't think about it. Grasping the bag like a lifeline, she covers her nose and mouth and breathes. She knows the drill by now. Eyes still closed, she concentrates – in . . . out . . . in . . . out . . . in . . . And it subsides, like it always does. Her muscles unknot themselves, her throat opens like a flower – until finally she can lower the bag. She will have to look at him now.

He has sat down opposite her, so as she opens her eyes, she finds she is looking straight into a face she recognises. The mid-brown hair has receded slightly. He has a day's growth of beard on his cheeks, which are thinner than she remembers. There are lines threaded round generous lips, pursed now, in concern. But the eyes – the eyes are the same – pools of melted chocolate, warm, liquid and focused entirely on her own. She is too taken aback to feel anything other than astonishment.

"Luke!"

"Hello Andrea."

"What . . . How . . . I thought you were in the Middle East somewhere!"

"I was. Just came back to – visit my parents." He glances away and the tension increases round his mouth.

Looking at him, she is back in school for a moment. It's their last day. They are sitting on the school field, arms touching, saying goodbye. "I'm coming back," he assures her. "It's only a year, and I'll write. I'll send you a postcard from every country – promise." He did send three or four – Mumbai, Kuala Lumpur, Brisbane – then, nothing. And he didn't come back – or if he did, it was when she'd gone to college. Her mum met his in Tesco and found out he'd landed a job with Lockheed in Riyadh, earning a fortune. Andrea had tried to move on.

As he looks back at her, she realises something which the therapist needs to know. She's not afraid of him! For the first time in nearly two years, she's sitting opposite a man and she's not afraid.

"I heard what happened." His voice is the same as she remembers, empathetic, warm, as chocolatey as his eyes.

"Oh." She can't hold his gaze. Don't think about it.

"How are you?"

"You know – getting there. I'm having some help." The guarded response slips out with force of habit, but she can feel the genuineness of his concern. For a second, she remembers the gentle voice asking the same question at school, when she was so concerned about her parents' pending divorce. He saw through her bravado and reached out to her inner self which was screaming with suppressed turmoil. He's doing it again now.

"Yes, Mum told me you couldn't go out after it happened – you had, what's it called – claustrophobia?"

"Agoraphobia." She still finds it difficult to say the word, but almost imperceptibly, and despite his broken promise to keep in touch, she is aware of the faint flutter of a forgotten trust.

"Well, you're here – so you must be getting over it."

"This is the first time – it's part of my treatment. I'm supposed to show the therapist the receipt to prove that I came – and I had to do it on my own."

"And you've done it. That's brilliant. They caught the guy, didn't they?"

Andrea gasps. Her stomach clenches again. She stares at Luke, waiting for the throat closure, the tears – but they don't come. She hears her own voice from a distance. "Yes – the therapist's trying to get me to the point where I can go to the court and testify by video link at his trial. I . . . I'm sorry, Luke – I can't talk about it any more – it makes the flashbacks worse . . . "

She's amazed she manages to tell him that much. Normally if anyone mentions The Crime, she freezes. None of the coping strategies work then. She can still feel the man's hands on her body, forcing her down, ripping, tearing, destroying . . .

"Sorry – that was a stupid question. If you do need to talk . . . But hey . . . " His voice tails off, embarrassed. "I did mean to keep writing, you know. I was going to come home. Life got in the way – there was this chance meeting in the States, a job offer – had to give it a go. Of course it's all gone pear-shaped now . . . " He stops abruptly, looking away again.

"What do you mean?" It's good to find she can still be interested in someone other than herself.

"It's a long, boring story – for another day, maybe? Perhaps we've all got things we don't talk about easily, eh? Look – your chocolate must be cold. How about I get us another one and we can talk about school – who you still see, who I still see – actually there isn't anyone, come to think of it. I was rubbish at keeping in touch."

"Love another chocolate, thanks. You can fill me in on the last ten years." It's still there – that warm fuzziness she remembers from a decade ago. She can feel it waking up inside her like a polar bear emerging from a long hibernation through a frozen winter.

They sit with their chocolate and Andrea is surprised by the return of a long forgotten sense of camaraderie. Months closeted in her room, watching life through a window, have paralysed her social instincts. Yet she finds herself laughing at tales of the camel races in the Saudi desert, which attract so many people that they drive along both sides of the dual carriageway and the central reservation, so people coming the other way have to swerve onto the shifting sands. She can picture the Toyota pickups with their cargos of goats and women. She can feel the dry, sand-laden breeze, hot as an electric fan, and smell the odours of the souk – rotting meat and stale sweat, mingled with that odd musky perfume peculiar to Arab women.

She talks about Before – when she had a life. Memories of her years at Durham University are relived. She tells him about her first job in a city publishing house, about her fantasies of authorial glory, conjured at the desk of a lowly editorial assistant. She talks about her house mates and . . . But that was the end of Before, so she stops abruptly and looks up.

That's when she spots Mum. She's sitting at a table near the front of the shop with a cup in front of her and a plate of crumbs. She's obviously been there for ages. Andrea had completely forgotten! Mum smiles and she smiles back. Luke turns round, and waves, so she clearly feels it's safe to come over.

"Luke – I heard you were home." She looks at Andrea, who knows she is taking in the flushed cheeks, eyes which have woken from a long sleep, the smile still lurking in the corners of the mouth. "Andrea, I've got an errand or two to run. How about if I come back in an hour, shall I – same place?"

Her daughter is about to agree when Luke interrupts. "It's OK, Mrs Emerson. Andrea – are you ready for an old mate to walk you home?"

Andrea hesitates momentarily. Could this be a step too far? It's her first test after all – she deserves a gold star though. "I might . . . "

"We can deal with it – I've still got the paper bag, remember."

She follows Luke to the door and into the roaring space outside, catching her breath. Then she looks at his face again, into the chocolate eyes, and takes his offered arm. It feels like the end of the beginning.

PEPPERMINT TEA

by Angela Haward

THE peppermint tea is too hot. Luke feels his lips stinging as he takes the first sip – he drinks it anyway. It needs to hurt. The taste is clean, antiseptic, just what he needs to flush out the filth in his mind. He deserves to feel pain – he always will.

He hasn't been in here for about three years. He sort of recognises the older woman wiping the tables, but the rather officious young manager and the foreign girl who had served him are strangers. The once familiar town is full of unknowns now. With a start, he realises he is a stranger himself. No-one greets him in the street like they used to. They've all left, dispersed around the globe like autumn leaves. Only he has come back to lick his wounds in the womb of his memory.

He doesn't even know why he's here. Maybe it's to hide from himself amidst the familiar English chatter, the clatter of crockery, the busyness of the daily round in this little suburban idyll. Only there isn't much chatter at this hour of the morning as the coffee rush hasn't yet begun. Or is it just another way to punish himself, surrounded as he is by the inescapable smell of coffee?

But he needs to think, away from his parents' barrage of questions, their well-intentioned smothering. He can't go on lying to them – the knots are getting too complex, but how to stop now? They keep asking if the office has given him a return date.

A loud and tinny version of Bohemian Rhapsody splinters the background sound. He'd meant to put the phone on silent. At least he's not at home so he can answer this time. Glancing at the name on the screen, he feels a pang of irritation. "Hello, Jean-Pierre . . ."

"Can you talk?" The voice on the other end is heavily accented.

"No – I'm in a coffee shop. I'll ring you back later, before I go home. Don't ring the house."

"Ze police 'ave been 'ere."

"They've got nothing on you. It's just scare tactics – they're trying to keep onside with the Saudis. Look, I'll call you later." Hastily cancelling the call, Luke feels a stirring of anger. It's about time Jean-Pierre took his share of guilt on those expensively clad shoulders. It was his house where it all kicked off.

The foreign girl is serving the next customer and an aroma of coffee drifts across the room. The customer's tray rattles and Luke shivers. Strong coffee and rattling cups – eight little beakers on a tray, dumped on the floor as the prisoners rolled up their bedding mats and jostled to use the bucket in the corner. The scent of coffee masks the stench of human ordure and the odour of unwashed male bodies – sensations all inextricably linked and filling the last eight months of Luke's life with secret memories.

He takes a large gulp of the tea in an effort to purge his mind. The picture refuses to fade. Write it down. That's the best way. He can treat it like work – bullet point it, hold a meeting with his parents, detach a bit. So – new pen and notebook from The Card Shop – OK let's see . . .

- Meet Jean-Pierre in Washington DC (youth hostel)
- J-P offers me work in Riyadh (influential dad etc)
- Move to Riyadh with Lockheed
- Good at job – frequent promotion – make a killing

They know all this. Luke realises he's just hedging. Perhaps he'll just hint at the hedonism of the expat lifestyle. He can feel the sweat prickle in his armpits as he remembers the parties, the illicit drink, easy sex with all those willing expat nurses, the drugs when someone came across the elusive dealer in the souk, the ever-present sense of danger because they all knew the dire consequences of being caught. He writes a couple more points.

- Parties
- Drink

That would do. On to the next . . .

- Landlord gave me notice to quit my apartment
- J-P invites me to move in with him temporarily (large house with pool etc)
- J-P goes home on leave. Left in charge of the house

He's getting to the nub of it now.

- Making drink in the cellar for the parties
- Raid by religious police
- Arrested and charged with alcohol offences
- Eight months in prison without trial
- Consul works to get me home
- Saudi and British Govs enter a period of *entente cordiale*
- Allowed home
- Lockheed fire me – bringing the company into disrepute

Luke is sweating profusely now. It looks so bland listed out like that. It doesn't explain why he wrote home every couple of weeks on consulate-supplied paper describing his job and his fictitious travels as if nothing was wrong. It doesn't explain why he told his parents he could no longer Skype or email them. It doesn't mention the horror of the prison cell, the frying heat of the exercise yard, the rancid food supplemented by consular supplies, the decreasing visits from former colleagues which stopped altogether in the end.

Looking up to clear his head, Luke's eye is caught by the latest customer at the till. Clutching her mug like a lifeline and with more than a hint of panic in her eyes she searches for somewhere to sit. He experiences a jolt of recognition which sets the adrenalin coursing round his body. It's Andrea! She hasn't changed much in ten years – thinner, maybe, blonde hair cut in a bob, face pale and bare of makeup. She looks . . . exposed.

She heads for the back of the shop, squeezing into the corner table, and glances round the room with doe-like trepidation, ready to make a dash for it at the least sign of threat.

Andrea Emerson – ex-girlfriend, reminder of an age of innocence, of the time before his rise and fall. Andrea Emerson, traumatised rape victim – his mother emailed him the link to the local paper. He had treated her like – well, like dirt, abandoning her for a better offer without so much as a backward glance. More amends to make, then. Should he go and speak to her now? No – what would he say? Hey, Andrea – sorry I didn't write, sorry I dropped you without a word, sorry you were attacked. But she looks so vulnerable, sitting there all alone – like a rabbit in the headlights. And he's in self-flagellation mode anyway.

Luke moves hesitantly towards the back of the room, tray in hand, and notices she is sucking the flake from her hot chocolate, eyes closed, smiling. He decides it may be better to sit near her rather than at her table. But as he deposits his tray, he is startled by her loud gasp followed by a painful struggle for breath. His initial thought is asthma, but then he realises this is a torment he has seen before – in the cell in Riyadh.

A man is fighting to breathe and crying as the guards pull him to the door. Guilty of theft, the barbarous Sharia law dictates he will lose a hand. The man's terror is palpable. Luke is powerless to intervene and the scene replays in his mind on a loop. He describes it to the consular representative who visits him later the same day. Revealing compassion unexpected in a politician, the man from the consulate leaves Luke a paper bag and tells him to get the man to breathe into it should the panic recur. But the man never comes back.

So – he knows what to do for Andrea, and he has a paper bag.

"Here, hold this over your mouth and breathe slowly. That's it. Just concentrate on breathing."

Andrea takes the bag wordlessly and, as she follows his instructions, the gasping breaths settle to a regular rhythm. Luke waits, watching her with concern. He wonders what else he can offer her. More hot chocolate, that would do it. Hot chocolate – comforting, warm, encouraging memories of the age of innocence when they first found one another. A pageant of their schooldays begins parading through his mind as he waits for their drinks at the counter . . . Andrea's laughter, her direct gaze, her courage after her parents' divorce, which masked a deep-seated need for reassurance. He finds himself wanting to sit with her, wanting her to return him to the time before her trauma and before his own.

Conversation is hesitant at first, rusty from disuse.

"How are you?" he asks – what a lame beginning.

She looks like a trampled flower, crushed and broken, as she gazes up at him. There is a defensiveness in her reply. "Oh, you know, getting there."

But, over their chocolate, he perseveres. That old desire to protect and nurture, which he remembers from school, is surfacing through the stagnant pool of his recent past. Gently, he encourages her to open up and, as they talk, he watches her unfold. Feeling her unacknowledged need to talk, he tries to draw her out about her trauma, aware that he could be walking on quicksand so soon after their reunion.

"They caught the guy, didn't they?" He watches her recoil, but then feels a sense of privilege as she struggles to talk about the rape, the agoraphobia which has dogged her ever since, her fear of men. Her candour takes them both by surprise.

Gradually, the reviving water of old friendship sees her begin to grow again. He is tempted to reveal his own fall from grace, but catches himself just in time. For the moment, he wants her to remember him as he was then, oozing adventurous idealism, not embittered by the fallout from crime and punishment.

Instead, he encourages the reminiscences. "Do you know what happened to Joanna Etherton?"

"Yes! She did go to Oxford, but she dropped out after a term and followed a boyfriend to Paris. I think she got a job as a croupier in some gambling den in the Latin Quarter! What happened to your mate, Jonathan?"

"God knows. Last I heard, he was working as an assistant stage manager at the repertory theatre in Weymouth. So much for RADA, then!"

As they relax into memories of their lives in the time *Before*, the knots in Luke's brain unravel a little. The dawning trust in Andrea's eyes makes his own truth seem marginally less shameful. Her eyes are as he remembers, blue and expressive, hesitant, fearful at first, then sparkling with interest and – yes, there it is – attraction . . .

"My Mum's over there." The spell is broken. Luke turns round to acknowledge the woman he remembers from hours spent over coffee in her kitchen after school. "I was supposed to meet her outside over an hour ago!"

Mrs Emerson leaves her table and makes her way through the shop towards them. Luke has seconds to decide where to go from here. He wants to hang onto this girl for longer. This feels like the beginning of a second chance for both of them. He has screwed up his life and hers has been screwed up for her. They are both damaged goods – but damage can be repaired, even if the mends are always visible.

"Can I walk you home, Andrea?" he asks quickly. He sees her hesitate, feels her fear. This is her first trip out, after all. Maybe it's too soon. It was rushing into something that got him into a mess in the first place.

He can read her eyes, anxiety, embarrassment, concern and – hope. She wants to walk with him. She does trust him, Luke who does not deserve any trust, Luke who let her down, who has lied to his family, who has fallen into a moral abyss from which he thought he may never emerge. He feels a great surge of longing. With her, it might just be possible to go back, to start from the beginning, to get it right – for both of them.

"OK – is that all right, Mum?"

Mrs Emerson hesitates, then smiles tactfully. "Yes, of course. I've got a few errands to run anyway. I'll see you at home. I'm on my mobile if you need me." She directs this last remark at Luke, as well as her daughter.

As they leave the shop, Luke offers Andrea his arm, knowing she may need some physical as well as emotional support. As she takes it, they share a glance of mutual understanding. Nothing is ever so broken that it can't be fixed. It just needs the right glue.

CAFÉ AU LAIT

by Liz Losty

MARIA thought the old lady in front of her looked like she was in a daze. Maybe she was daydreaming. Maybe she had Alzheimer's or one of those other diseases where you lose your marbles and you don't know where you are anymore. Maria felt a little alarmed and decided the best option was to repeat herself – but just speak a lot louder this time.

"Cappuccino, Espresso, Ristretto, Americano, Latte or Flat White, madam?" She decided to point to the large menu board behind her as well, as if to emphasise the choice available. She felt like a weather girl on TV, standing there sweeping her arm up and down the menu board, imagining herself in a designer dress with shiny hair and perfect makeup, standing in front of a weather map on the TV news.

Maria often liked to pretend she was on TV when she was serving in the coffee shop. She would chat confidently to the customers, trying to imitate their accents so she could improve her spoken English as much as possible, calling everyone 'sir' or 'madam' and giving them her winning smile. Maybe she could get on TV, on one of those reality shows. They had done reality shows on airports, Essex, Newcastle and countless 'police on patrol' shows: why not a reality TV show in a coffee shop? They could focus on the pretty young girl with the cute Nordic accent and winning smile who worked there (Maria also starred in her own daydreams) and the wide range of clientele, the cross section of society represented by a local coffee shop. The customers all have their own stories, their own personalities, and the reality TV programme would feature a couple of real characters before focusing back on Maria. All the customers would describe her with great fondness and praise her friendliness, Scandinavian good looks and welcoming smile while puzzling over the fact that she was still single and not yet a star. Maria wondered if she would be allowed to control some of the script for the show.

The young couple behind the old lady tutted and looked at Maria, who snapped to and addressed the old lady again. "Madam, you know what kind of coffee you want?" she asked testily.

The old lady looked bewildered at the choice and peered at the foreign words on the large menu board behind Maria. "Just a coffee please, a black coffee with some cold milk, just a normal coffee please."

"That is Americano. Drink here? Or you want take away?" Maria pointed to the tower of cardboard cups behind her.

"Well, yes please, I do want to drink my coffee here. Where else would I drink it?" The old lady's baffled reply unnerved Maria but she pressed on.

"Small, medium, large?" Maria asked, in what she hoped was a brusque, business-like manner. She wanted to convey to the young couple next in the queue that her obvious efficiency meant she was not the cause of the delay and the long queue now forming.

"Just a small black coffee, with some milk, in a china cup with a saucer, to drink while I sit at one of the tables in this café," the old lady replied.

"So you want small Americano, cold milk, drink in," Maria said.

The old lady nodded and smiled, hoping the test was over and that *somehow* she had passed. "That is £2.40 please," said Maria. The old lady paused, shocked by the price, then fumbled in her handbag, pushing tissues and medications out of the way until she found her little change purse and carefully counted out the money with a nervous hand.

"That should be it exactly, dear," she said as she pushed the coins across the counter to Maria.

"Next please, what I get you?" Maria asked the couple behind the old lady, who turned to look at the couple and then looked back at Maria, obviously confused.

***

"Excuse me madam, here is your Americano." The old lady hadn't taken much notice of the young man busying himself beside the hissing and steaming machine next to Maria. He pointed at a tray with a cup, saucer and milk jug. "Your coffee, madam." She wished they knew her name, and would prefer to be addressed as Mrs Bennett, or even Margaret, which would seem friendlier than this constant curt address of 'madam'. It somehow felt like an admonishment.

"Oh, right, thank you." Margaret picked up the tray and smiled her thanks at the young man. Finally! She sat down at the nearest free table she could find.

Breathing a sigh of relief, she felt that she had passed the test. She had actually managed to go into a coffee shop, decipher a menu and go through endless rounds of questions, just so she could have a cup of coffee. She smiled to herself, amused at the rigmarole, as her mother would have called it.

She took her first sip of a very average cup of coffee. It tasted nowhere near as good as the *café au lait* she had drunk just before the war at *Les Deux Magots* in Paris. Her thoughts turned to that wartime, occupied city, a world at war, people fearing for their lives and yet somehow they'd been able to make a decent cup of coffee in less than five minutes and with far fewer questions and far more smiles.

Europe had been at war for less than a year and no-one had really thought Paris would fall so quickly. There were many tears of fear, shame and despair on that summer's day in June 1940 when the German army marched past the Arc de Triomphe.

If Paris could be occupied so quickly where would it end? It felt like the entire world was on the brink of destruction.

And then there was Margaret, and there were many like her. She had grown up in the security of a loving family from the Home Counties. She had spent many happy summers in a holiday home in Le Touquet which the family shared with their French cousins. She had even spent one summer touring France with her favourite Parisian cousin, Estelle. Her French was fluent, her memory perfect, her intelligence honed by an excellent education and a passion for crosswords and puzzles. She was perfect. The work was dangerous, they left her in no doubt of the risks, and she soon learnt that none of the horrors had been exaggerated. But while fear froze the souls of many, it had put steel into Margaret. She was more determined than afraid, and more defiant than cowed.

She remembered the many colleagues she had met on her missions. She was warned never to think of anyone as a friend and to trust no-one. Yet there had been one she did trust. It was against all orders, but she was guided by her instinct. Their love had been brief, but with all the intensity that war forces into the hearts of lovers.

Margaret felt dreamlike with the memories that she was now visiting, years later, sitting in a coffee shop a world away from the Paris at war she had lived in. She instinctively fingered the small gold pendant she wore around her neck, a *fleur de lys*. She still missed him, all these years later. He had given it to her before they parted. Unknown to either of them it was to be his last mission.

He had never come back. She had cried alone. But he had always told her that, no matter what happened, she must remember that no-one would ever have the love they had. She had started to cry when he said that as they lay in bed that last evening. He knew he had to change her mood; he couldn't leave her crying. He gently dabbed her cheek with his thumb to stop the tears travelling any further. "Remember, we will always have Paris," he said. Even then it was such a funny line, not romantic, just silly. "But the Germans have Paris, that's the problem," she said, smiling sadly. "Yes, but not for long and certainly not for ever." And the steel in her core turned and shone at his words.

Margaret's mouth formed into a soft smile while she remembered how they had looked at each other silently and then kissed. And both had offered up a silent prayer that he would be right, and that Paris – and the world – would soon be free.

He was right of course. The Germans didn't have Paris for ever, the war was won, peace was restored, and no-one would ever have the love that they had. She smiled sadly when she thought of all that he had fought for and never lived to see.

***

Maria looked over at Margaret and saw her smiling absently. 'That old woman, she got the crazies,' Maria thought to herself. She wondered if she would allow her to appear in her reality TV show but the old lady probably didn't even know what the real world was, never mind reality TV.

ICED CRUSH

by Richard Hopgood

"A DECAF regular cap," the man said "and a raspberry milkshake." The man was stocky, tanned, with thick eyebrows and a square jaw. She looked down at the small boy clutching the man's hand. His large blue eyes looked anxious.

"You like some food? A delicious cake for the boy?" Elizaveta asked with a tight smile.

"You hungry Matt? Maybe your Mum was too busy to get you breakfast . . . "

The boy pursed his lips and shook his head. The man looked at Elizaveta's name badge.

"Where you from, Elizabeth?"

"Riga. In Latvia," she replied. "You should visit, very beautiful city . . . " She felt his eyes measuring her up, lingering on her blonde hair.

"Funny, you look sort of Swedish. Or Finnish." He grinned, as if defining her sexually, and tugged the boy behind him to the cash desk. Elizaveta suppressed her irritation. Nobody ever seemed interested in Latvia, apart from old people who had been on a Baltic cruise.

She felt for the boy. He was a few years older than her own daughter, Elise, who was living with her mother on the Baltic coast. She hoped Elise was having a better morning than the small boy, who seemed ill at ease with his father. Maybe his parents were getting divorced, or not getting along. Quite a few dads had come in this half-term week and she could usually tell which were separated: they were too happy, or too irritable, with not much in between. Some men did not seem to discover they liked being dads until it was too late . . .

Elizaveta had been in England for six months now. Her friend, Olga, worked in London in a shipping firm which did a lot of business in the Baltic. She had stayed in Olga's flat for a few weeks while she looked for work and a room, but she had been told at an interview that her English was 'not up to scratch'. The fact that she had a degree in English from Riga University cut no ice. Olga then found an English boyfriend and asked Elizaveta to move out. So she had contacted another Latvian friend, and ended up with a room and a job in the coffee shop. Not exactly what she had dreamed of when she came to England, but it was a start, and she had been able to send some money to her mother, which made her feel a little better. And her colloquial English was improving.

"Smile!" a voice hissed behind her. It was Maria's way of warning her that the boss was on the prowl. "Always look happy," he would say. "It's infectious. Smile and the world smiles with you." She did her best to smile each time she served somebody, but it was hard work, and sometimes her face ached from the effort. The English women, she noted, rarely smiled in return and nor did their husbands if they were with them. Men without women always smiled, but usually for the wrong reasons. She found it rather insulting.

A small queue was building up. A woman with two children insisted on answering her mobile while Elizaveta waited for her order, gesturing to the board as if pinpointing her choice with a laser gun while her children rummaged amongst the biscuits.

"Keep the tempo up," her boss said quietly behind her. "The natives will get fractious otherwise."

She shrugged resignedly as the woman finally finished her phone call. "I said a skinny latte. Didn't you hear?" she said sharply, whilst pulling her daughter's hands away from a chocolate chip cookie.

"You were on the phone," Elizaveta stammered.

"I'm so sorry, madam, we'll get that immediately," her boss cut in, moving Elizaveta to one side. She moved sulkily to the coffee machine to pour the drink. He stayed to take the rest of the order, and only allowed Elizaveta back to her station when the woman had moved further down the counter.

"Never argue with a customer," he whispered into her ear. "Next time, it's a warning."

Elizaveta found it humiliating. These rude young mothers with their designer clothes and obsessive preening. When they were not on the phone, they were swiping the screens and tapping out messages with their long varnished nails or having idiotic conversations with other mothers while their children were left to amuse themselves. Did they not realise what a privilege it was to have children and to be with them? She imagined her daughter, Elise, sitting at one of the tables with her mother, wearing the pink dress her mother had made for her and carrying the little white bag Elizaveta had bought for her when she last went home. They would be sitting there waiting for her to finish her shift so they could go the park. Elise loved the swings. She felt herself pushing the swing and watching Elise ascend in an arc towards the sky before swinging back with a delighted squeal, shouting "Higher! Higher!" and catching the swing as it came back, just at the end of its return, and firmly pushing Elise skywards again. That was her role, she thought, to push Elise towards the sky and happiness, but always to be ready to catch her when she came to earth again.

Her dreams of Elise always foundered on taking her home. 'Home' was a room in an old lady's house, where she lived for what passed as a low rent in return for doing the shopping, walking an ancient black terrier, making the supper and cleaning the whole house once a week. When she was not working, she kept to her room because otherwise she knew the old lady would have her doing jobs the whole time. Elizaveta did not eat with Mrs Parsons because she could not bear the noise of the old woman chewing and swallowing, or the caustic remarks she made about her cooking. She told Mrs Parsons she was on a diet. To save money, she existed largely on sandwiches or cakes from the coffee shop which would otherwise be put out with the rubbish. "Doesn't seem to be working, dear, does it?" Mrs Parsons observed sardonically.

She had mentioned Elise to Mrs Parsons, who had said her daughter would be welcome to stay – for a day or two. Elizaveta had told her mother she shared a house with a nice old lady but she knew what it would be like if Elise came. After the initial novelty had worn off, Mrs Parsons would expect Elizaveta to run around for her as if Elise did not exist. In Mrs Parsons' eyes, that was the deal. Elizaveta was there to 'do' for her. Mrs Parsons imagined that Elizaveta was used to Communist squalor, and that being in such a smart house in an elegant area was a big step up for her, a stroke of good fortune for which she should be eternally grateful. It was lucky that Mrs Parsons had a heart of gold. She could easily have asked for more rent.

Elizaveta's weekends were very boring unless her boyfriend, Jan, was passing near London. He was a lorry driver from Warsaw. When she met him, he drove all over Europe, down to the Balkans and Turkey, and over to Germany and Holland. She thought there was something heroic about travelling to such remote places. She had always had a thing about long distance journeys. Maybe it was watching the ships coming into the docks at Riga and sailing off into the open sea. But airports and even stations were just as magical. She loved to look down the departure boards, savouring the names of far-off cities. A few times she had accompanied Jan, but the reality of long hours on motorways had disappointed her. One motorway was pretty much like another. And Jan did not have a great store of conversation, beyond work and how he could save enough to buy his own wagon one day; and country and western music, which he played relentlessly. Having sex in the cab of a lorry with Jim Reeves crooning in the background was not her idea of fun, or romance for that matter.

Usually Jan was on a tight schedule, so he would meet her in a car park in town, and they would drive out to a layby near the M25. Once he drove her to a service station and they had burger and chips and a cola, which he paid for. But mostly they had sex, and then chatted briefly, and had coffee from his flask, until it was time for him to drop her back again. She returned to Mrs Parsons feeling somehow shamed. It was not the life she wanted, and she told nobody about Jan, not even her own mother. Mrs Parsons often joked when she returned from an outing, "Been to see your Prince Charming have you?" 'As if,' Elizaveta thought bitterly.

She dreamed that one day she would meet a doctor. He would be of a higher culture than the average man who came into the coffee shop; and he would be attracted to her mind and not just her blonde hair. He would have a big house in the country, with tall iron gates and a gravel drive, and he would spend most of his time doing life-saving operations, like heart transplants and brain surgery. She felt it would be heroic to work in the NHS, but he would support her through medical school to become a plastic surgeon. Her fabulous income would ensure their life style was not compromised by his idealism. She would have a practice in Harley Street, which was full of wonderful white houses. In time, she might even have her own TV series. Her mother would be very proud of her. Best of all, Elise could come to live with her permanently. She would have her own nursery, and a governess to attend to her care and education. Every Saturday, she and Elise would go clothes shopping, in Bond Street, and return home with smart bags bearing the legends 'London, Paris, St Petersburg'. A frisson of delight stole over her when she thought about it.

She often wondered how she would recognise 'her' doctor when he finally came in, and how they might strike up a relationship. She was sure it would happen, a prophecy of future happiness and rescue. Only the details bothered her as to how mutual recognition and attraction would occur. She was sure he would be single, but sometimes she imagined him coming in with another woman, a girlfriend or even worse a wife. He would be very unhappy, maybe that was it, she would feel his great sorrow, and he would feel hers and an electricity of compassion and desire would flow between them. The girlfriend or wife would have to take the hint; his career depended on it. People's lives hung on his finding the right woman, to love and support him. If they really loved him, they should let him go.

Alas no doctors had come in so far, apart from the young GP who had examined her rash. He was not the man she was waiting for. He had told her to eat fewer cakes and avoid steamed milk. 'Stupid boy,' she thought.

Despite all the customers she served, and the smiles she dutifully exchanged, it seemed very hard to actually meet anybody. She could not leave her post unless it was her break, and the manager discouraged conversations with customers which held up the queue. Only once had it happened. A smart young man called Terry, dressed in a blue blazer with an impressive badge, white shirt and tie had ordered breakfast, put a large tip in the jar and insisted on buying her a drink. "Your smile has lit up my morning," he said. The manager was out that morning so she had taken the money for a blue iced crush. He had then invited her to his table. Maria had said "Go for it", so she had sat with him for ten minutes and sipped her drink. Terry was in the holiday business. He owned a string of travel shops. He was doing some informal market research on people's holiday dreams, he said, and had decided to focus on customers in the classier coffee shops. "Full of B1s and C2s," he said, explaining that these were generally people with high disposable incomes but not much imagination about how to spend it. What he really wanted was to interview them when they got back from their unexciting holidays, and persuade them to raise their sights and visit one of his shops. They would never regret it. The only trouble was reaching them. He could hardly wander around the shop, disturbing people's conversations. The manager would probably ask him to leave. Far better to approach people in their own homes. He noticed that Elizaveta got people to sign up for loyalty cards. She must overhear people talking about their forthcoming holidays. If she got people to give their addresses when they signed a loyalty card, could she not give him a ring, or even text him, with the addresses of those going on holiday? If they visited his shop and bought a holiday, he'd give her a five per cent commission – on a £2,000 holiday, that was £100. Not bad eh? Then he had slipped her a business card with his telephone number.

It had only happened twice. When the manager was away, she had signed up four customers, with their addresses, and asked them if they were off on holiday soon. Then she had texted two addresses to Terry. It all seemed very simple. She imagined the families talking on another occasion of the wonderful holidays which Terry's firm had arranged for them, so superior to the boring vacations they had experienced before, and such good value! And she would feel five crisp £20 notes in her handbag, which would help pay for her own holiday on the Baltic coast with her mother and Elise. Good things did sometimes happen.

A few weeks later the first family returned to the coffee shop looking very disgruntled. They had come home, she heard them say, to find the back door open and the house ransacked. The plasma TV and the woman's jewellery were gone – and some valuable antiques. The insurance settlement would run into thousands.

"I asked the policeman how on earth they knew we had gone on holiday," the young mother said. "I mean, the car was outside and the lights and TV were programmed to go on and off. He said somebody must have overheard something, and maybe followed me back. Gives me the creeps."

Elizaveta listened, aghast.

"Anyway, they think they know who did it. They just need to make some enquiries about how he found out we were on holiday, in case he has an accomplice."

At that moment, the coffee shop door opened, and two uniformed policemen approached the counter.

Elizaveta's blood ran cold.

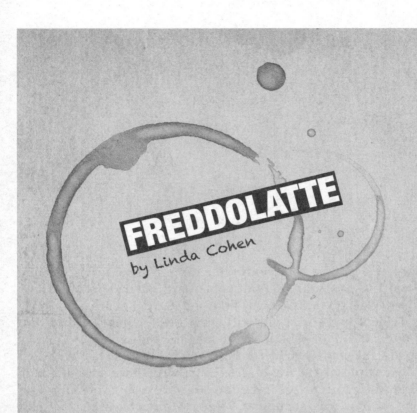

FREDDOLATTE

by Linda Cohen

EDNA knew it must be serious. Her three children were coming over on Tuesday to take her out, something that had not happened before. "We'll go to that lovely little coffee shop near you, Mum," Lucy, her eldest, had said. Edna had never been to a coffee shop and none of her children ever bothered to take her out.

Come to think of it, when was the last time any of them had bothered to visit? Even a phone call was a rare occurrence. Once a month Sam, her second child, rang to see if she was still alive. He barely stayed on the phone for more than a minute. "Hello, Mum. OK, are you?" and, without stopping to find out exactly how she was, went on to tell her how busy he was, how he'd just about managed to find a minute to phone but couldn't stay on the line long as he was expecting a very important transatlantic call which he couldn't miss.

In the background Edna could always hear his snooty wife, Jayne, barking orders to their latest *au pair*, usually something about had she finished the ironing yet, because the silver had to be tackled next. 'Stuck up cow,' thought Edna. Who did she think she was? Just because Sam had been so successful in his City job she had assumed the role of Lady of the Manor and drifted around the house as if she was royalty. Edna couldn't stand her, especially after she had started spelling her name with a Y and insisting that everyone knew she was Jayne, not Jane. When Sam first met her she was quite happy being just Miss Jane Smythington. After Sam was more successful and they got married, she became Jayne Smythington-Worth. She felt it gave her more of an edge of county respectability, but Edna thought she was just plain stuck up.

Lucy was not much better. 'Condescending,' thought Edna. She had not seen her daughter for three months. "I'm studying for an Open University degree, so I have very little time at the moment. One should always try and better oneself, you know. Maybe you and Dad should have done more, travelled a bit, seen more friends, taken up bridge, then perhaps you wouldn't be so lonely now."

But Edna and Reg had been happy in their cosy little world. They hadn't needed friends, or travel, or education. The garden and allotment filled their hours. Reg was never happier than when his cabbages and carrots came up and his lawn was mowed, especially when Edna pottered out with a cup of tea and a slice of cake and they admired his handiwork together. "Hollyhocks, Edna, hollyhocks and vegetables. That's the secret to happiness," Reg used to say, and they'd laugh together. Now that was all gone. Her darling Reg had died eighteen months ago. No more cabbages, and certainly no hollyhocks.

Eve, her youngest, was always trying to 'find herself'. She was just back from two months in India where she had lived in a tent with like-minded people, surviving on one meal a day of rice and vegetables, a vow of silence, and meditation. Edna thought she had probably not found herself yet because she had come back more miserable than ever and was now planning to go to a retreat in Scotland to live among the sheep, practise yoga three times a day, and weave baskets. She believed colonic irrigation was on the programme as well – perhaps that would do it, thought Edna.

Anyway today was the day: the three of them were on their way, and something told Edna that things did not bode well.

They all arrived together in Sam's BMW. Edna watched them get out the car, Sam hurrying them up the path. (He probably had another transatlantic call due at any moment.) They stood, looking up at the house as if sizing up what it would be worth, before Lucy knocked on the door. Edna took a few moments to get there, her Zimmer frame going before her. "Hello Mum," they all said together.

"Why aren't you ready yet?" asked Eve, irritably. "You know we're going out for coffee. Where's your coat and hat?" Edna felt herself being hurried along. Someone plonked her felt hat on top of her head while someone else thrust her arms in her tweed coat, none too gently. An air of being rushed by her three impatient children soon spoilt the feel-good factor Edna had tried to manufacture. 'That scowl on Eve's face could turn the milk sour,' Edna thought.

"We'll take you in the wheelchair, Mum," said Sam. "It's only down the road, no need to take the car." Edna would have loved a car ride. It had been so long since she had been in one, but she obediently got in the chair that Sam was already pushing out the front door and off they all went. It was a cold October day, made colder by the reception she had got from her three children. Not one of them had even given her a peck on the cheek. She sighed sadly to herself, and wondered what this meeting was all about.

Once inside the coffee shop her spirits lifted a little. It was quite busy. One of the tables was taken up by what she assumed was a grandfather and his delightful little granddaughter. They were so engrossed in each other – it was lovely to see. Edna remembered the days when Lucy's youngest used to come and spend the school holidays with her and Reg. They loved spoiling her, but that had stopped long ago. She couldn't blame them. After all, young people needed other young people and she was sure old people were boring to them. Nevertheless she missed seeing her grandchildren so much.

They wheeled Edna to the nearest table, and she looked around with interest. There was a young girl with a sweet face, but Edna thought she looked troubled and wondered what the matter was. She watched a nice young man hesitate at her table then engage her in conversation, and Edna wondered whether they knew each other. The girl had looked startled when the man approached her, and Edna felt worried for her, but wouldn't it be wonderful, she thought, if this was the start of a new romance? Edna would be in at the beginning! 'That's the trouble,' she thought. 'I'm always daydreaming. My Reg was always telling me off for that, but I always like people to be in pairs just like me and Reg were.' She sighed sadly, then couldn't help noticing the man was giving the girl a paper bag. 'What's that for?' she thought. The girl looked agitated. Edna hoped the young man wasn't bothering her and wondered if she should step in and say something. She was stopped in her tracks by Sam appearing and Eve telling her to stop staring at people. Edna felt embarrassed, as if she was encroaching on their private space. It really did show that she didn't go out much now, she thought sadly.

"Right, what's everyone having?" asked Sam in an over-jovial voice.

"Where's the menu?" asked Edna.

"There is no menu," said Lucy, "It's all written up on a blackboard there, see?" Edna looked around. Fancy not having any menus! How could that be? How could you choose what you wanted? "It's all up there, Mum, on the board. Americano, macchiato, flat white, iced coffee, freddolatte, steamers . . . "

Edna, not wanting to appear ignorant, said the first thing she could remember. "I'll have a Freddylater please." Macchiato sounded like something you caught off a lavatory seat, so she didn't fancy having one of them. She hoped her children would be proud of her if she ordered a Freddylater and that they would never guess she hadn't a clue what it was.

"Right," said Sam. "I'll just go and give the barista our order."

'Barrister?' thought Edna. 'Why would a barrister work in a coffee shop? They work in Law Courts.' She wondered if she dared ask her children, but decided not to. It was all too confusing.

"Now Mum," started Lucy, "we've brought you here today to discuss the fact that we all feel it would be in your best interests to think about a move. After all, you aren't getting any younger and, as you know, there have been a few incidents that your neighbours have reported to us. It's starting to be a worry."

"Move?" asked Edna. "Why would I move? Where would I move to?"

"Well," said Sam, "most people of your age have started to think about going into a home by now."

"After all," interrupted Eve, "you could lock yourself out of the house like Mrs Morris from two doors away did the other day, out in the street in nothing more than her slippers and nightie. And I worry that you could leave chops or something under the grill and fall asleep. We've all heard about incidents like that and we feel it would be in your best interests, for your safety . . . "

"We've made a few enquiries, and we've seen a lovely place," continued Lucy. "Rose Cottage, it's called. Just a few streets away from here, all mod cons, lovely rooms, you'd have company your own age and everything you need. Most of all, Mum, you would be safe and looked after."

There, it was out – the reason they had visited her after all these months was just so they could shove her into a home. Edna felt a tear roll down her cheek and she looked up to see a kindly middle-aged lady cleaning the table next to theirs. Beryl, her name tag read. 'She looks like a Beryl,' thought Edna, 'all comforting and gentle.' She wondered whether Beryl had children or a husband at home. She hoped so. Beryl looked such a kind lady. Edna knew Beryl had seen the tear escape and she felt uncomfortable. She didn't want people feeling sorry for her so she tried to cheer up, telling herself that no-one could make her do anything she didn't want to do. Besides, Beryl's smile of encouragement gave Edna the strength to say what she had wanted to say for years.

Sam had brought over a tray with the drinks. "Cappuccino for you, Eve, and for you, Lucy. A Freddolatte for you, Mum, and an espresso with two shots for me. Boy do I need this . . . " he said. Turning to Lucy he whispered, "This is going to be harder than I imagined. However will we be able to persuade her that she can no longer look after herself?"

Lucy had to agree. Turning away from her mother, she replied. "And now the neighbours are getting worried about her, it means we'll have to start taking much more interest. Quite honestly, none of us has the time to deal with all the problems she's causing."

"I may be old but I'm not deaf! I heard what you said." Edna's indignant tone made Sam soften his voice.

"Mum," said Sam, "it really is in your best interests. We can't keep looking after you ourselves. Jayne would love to, of course, but she has her charity committees and her board of school governors to deal with. What with that and her golf and bridge commitments – well there aren't enough hours in the day."

"Is that Jane with a Y?" asked Edna.

"What?" asked Sam.

"You know Jayne with a Y, not just Jane as in Jane."

Sam blushed. "What do you mean, Mum?" But of course he knew exactly what Edna meant.

"Jayne with a Y would no sooner look after me than she would swap her Mercedes for a bicycle," said Edna. "And Lucy. When was the last time you ever asked me over to your house for a meal, let alone a cup of tea or to see your kids? And Eve. You are so busy trying to 'find yourself' – I'm worried that when you do eventually find yourself you won't actually like what you find."

There was a stunned silence around the table. When Edna looked up, she noticed that the grandfather and the little girl had stopped talking together and were both staring at Edna's table, as were several people at other tables. She realised she had been shouting at her family, but felt strangely elated. She lowered her voice and, trembling, told them to please take her home now. "How dare you!" she hissed. "You take all this time to come and see me – no visits in between, no proper telephone calls – only to tell me that you are going to put me in a home. You should be ashamed of yourselves."

Sam, Lucy and Eve stood up together and, with very red faces, aware that the whole coffee shop was looking at them, started to gather their things together. "This is a conversation to be continued at home," said Sam in a strained voice. They started to wheel Edna hurriedly out of the shop.

As she drew level with the counter Edna looked at the young person pouring the coffees. 'Is that what they look like?' thought Edna. Nothing like the barristers she'd seen on the telly, that was for sure.

"Do you know?" she said, in a very loud voice that carried throughout the shop. "Do you know? It's disgusting. My Freddylater or whatever it's called was COLD. Whoever heard of cold coffee?"

BLACK AMERICANO

by Chris Payne

TRACY touched the 'End call' button on her phone and stared at the blank screen in disbelief. Susannah had done it again. Tracy had lost count of the times her sister-in-law's oh-so-reasonable voice had calmly destroyed her plans.

"I just don't think it's a good idea, Trace, that's all. Maisie's still very vulnerable and she needs a lot of love and affection right now. Dad's just arrived and I don't want to get in the way of their time together. If you'd just let me know you were coming out this way today . . . but it will have to be another time. And no, you can't talk to her; she's out with Dad."

"OK, I get it. Grandfather trumps aunt. I know when I'm beaten," Tracy stated sarcastically.

"No-one's beaten, Tracy, it's just a statement of fact. Dad isn't here often and she needs his attention."

"I give her attention," Tracy stormed silently at the phone's blank screen. "I give her love and affection. And I give her what you and my wet-fish brother never gave her: I give her ambition, a sense of purpose, and the skills to survive in a hostile world. Love and affection don't take you to the top, Susannah. They don't take you where I've got to."

She didn't need to have this argument out loud with Susannah any more. They'd had the conversation so often that it lay underneath every word they exchanged. Even in her sister-in-law's silence Tracy could hear the judgement Susannah would never voice again: "At what cost, Tracy? At what cost?"

'Cost, shmost,' Tracy's inner monologue mocked childishly. She had known what her sister-in-law was referring to. Susannah had always masked her envy of Tracy's relationship-free life with a coating of pity. After all, what did Susannah have to be proud of? Tracy's brother hadn't exactly been ambition's poster child. 'Big deal,' thought Tracy. 'Anyone can get married, anyone can procreate. Congratulations. But not anyone can do what I've done.'

It had been clear in Susannah's eyes from the first time Patrick brought her to Tracy's apartment to celebrate their engagement. During the tour, Susannah had exclaimed appropriately at the view, the cleverly recessed TV cabinet and the original artwork on the white walls. Back in the living room, though, Susannah had slipped off her shoes and tucked her legs underneath her on the leather couch, entwining her hand with Patrick's. "It's an awfully big place for just one person, isn't it?" she'd asked.

"I like big," Tracy had replied, pouring the champagne into crystal flutes.

"And I suppose when you get married and have children, you'll need the room," Susannah had continued. Tracy could still hear Patrick's nervous laughter in response. "Tracy have children? She'd never do anything that messy, would you sis?"

Tracy had smiled back at his sweet, weak face and nodded. But throughout the evening, Patrick and Susannah's hopeful enthusiasm for starting a family immediately had started Tracy thinking. Perhaps there was something in what they said: "The chance to give a child the kind of childhood we never had." Tracy could see the appeal in that, not enough to think about sharing her space or her financial success, but a germ of an idea had been planted.

Patrick and Susannah were true to their promise with such speed that Tracy suspected the child might have created the marriage as much as being the product of it. As soon as her brother had phoned to say that he and Susannah had had a baby girl, in a flash Tracy had seen the future. Susannah and Patrick wanted to give the child a different upbringing, but as far as they were concerned this just meant a lot of bleating about love and stability. They hadn't made any concrete plans: that's where Tracy could help. This little girl would have all the advantages Patrick and Tracy hadn't had. For Maisie, there would be no fighting her way through the local comprehensive, no joining the Navy because there was no money to waste time at university. Maisie would have a privileged upbringing but, with help from her street-smart auntie, she'd also know how to fight. Tracy could see it all.

So over the last seven years it had been increasingly baffling that Susannah and Patrick didn't seem to see it her way. Patrick melted into the background whenever his daughter's upbringing was discussed. He'd had a lifetime of avoiding battles with Tracy and his goal had always been a peaceful life. Susannah, though, was willing to discuss with infuriating reasonableness for hours on end, yet Tracy seldom emerged the winner. They had had their biggest fight ever over Maisie's schooling. Tracy hadn't been able to believe her ears when Susannah announced that Maisie would be going to a nursery group at the village hall, which was a feeder for the church-run primary. And worse, they had no intention of moving her to Connington House when her schooling started properly, not even at secondary school age!

"Not a believer in private education, my eye," Tracy had muttered under her breath. Of course cost was the issue. Even when Tracy had made it clear that she would pay for it all, Susannah remained obdurate. She made no objection to Tracy's visits, and even let her take Maisie off on whatever activities Tracy deemed necessary, but that was as far as Tracy's influence could stretch.

Tracy had poured all her energy into the activities. She spent countless hours researching on the internet for a combination of intellectually and physically stimulating entertainment appropriate to Maisie's age. They went to museums, to the theatre and the ballet; they had afternoon tea and went to an exercise class. "*Body Pump* for a four-year-old, Trace? Are you sure?" Susannah had murmured irritatingly. And maybe it hadn't been the most successful of their expeditions, but Tracy was a strong believer in starting physical fitness early.

Patrick's death had come as a shock. A heart attack was unforeseeable in one so young. At his funeral, Tracy had put her arm around Maisie and said "Family is what counts at a time like this. Without your Dad, you're the only family I've got – we'll be seeing a lot more of each other

70

from now on." She'd planted a red lipstick kiss on the weeping girl's head to seal the bargain.

In the months since the funeral, though, her access to Maisie seemed to have diminished. Susannah was always polite on the phone but, whatever date Tracy picked, it transpired that Maisie was busy. Today she'd tried a new strategy. Knowing it was half-term and that Susannah would be struggling to balance her work and childcare commitments, Tracy was sure she'd welcome a surprise chance to send Maisie out for a few hours.

"It's not like I have time for this," Tracy fumed and tucked her phone back into her glossy black handbag. Tracy would have to think of a new enticement, something Susannah really couldn't refuse. She was out of the office now anyway; maybe she should spend some time on that now.

She could see Susannah's local coffee shop across the street. She'd sworn not to go back there after that stupid waitress had refused to honour the café's own promotion of free refills. Still, at least they made a decent cup of coffee. Tracy strode across the street, pointing her key fob over her shoulder to lock the car and adroitly avoiding the puddles in her high-heeled boots. The steamy, scent-laden air of the coffee shop hit her in a welcome wave after the chill outside. She clicked briskly over to the counter without glancing left or right, but could tell from the noise that the place was busy.

Tracy was always amazed at how it survived. No staff on the till. She drummed her scarlet nails on the countertop with Susannah's voice still echoing in her head. Susannah had mentioned her father. What was his name again? She'd met him at the funeral, seen past his condolences that he was eyeing her with an interest inappropriate for the circumstances. He was old enough to be her father, too, for Christ's sake. Still she had not been as rude to him as she could justifiably have been. Even while mourning her brother, she'd realised that his in-laws could be a route to her niece's affections. So she'd returned his smiles and accepted his platitudes, filing the encounter away for future reference. She brought his face up in her mind. He was as bland and forgettable as his daughter. Tracy couldn't stand the thought of his live-and-let-live philosophy being the one that her niece was brought up with.

It was time to take action, Tracy decided. She'd driven all the way out here, to this godforsaken town her brother had called home. In order for the trip not to be a complete waste of time, she had to do something. If only she could have had some time alone with Maisie. Maybe it was worth sitting outside their house in the car and catching the little girl when she returned from her outing. Surely she was old enough now to keep secrets; they could organise a coded way of keeping in touch.

Tracy gazed idly into the mirror behind the counter as she continued to wait to be served. There were mirrors everywhere in this place. It was probably supposed to make it look bigger, but when it was crowded, like now, the effect was more like a day at the Harrods' sale, with bodies everywhere. Suddenly, Tracy stiffened. She recognised one happy couple at a table in the back. They hadn't noticed her. Oblivious to anyone but each other, they just looked like a contented grandfather and granddaughter. But to Tracy, they were thwarted desire.

Tracy's lips curved in a smile. She looked at her own reflection and used her fingers to tousle her fringe into a softer arrangement. She licked a finger and smoothed two sharp points in front of each ear. She tugged down her white blouse and straightened her shoulders. Never slow to recognise opportunity, this one was coming on a plate. Returning her attention to the serving counter, she realised that a staff member had approached and was watching her silently. Tracy showed no surprise – Tracy never showed surprise – and placed her order firmly. "Black Americano," she said. "With an extra shot." She was going to need a boost to take this conversation where it needed to go.

DOUBLE ESPRESSO

by Lesley Close

DENIS woke up to the sound of his granddaughter Maisie singing outside the bedroom door. He called out "Good morning, Maisie-bird," the words which meant she could come in.

She bounced on to the bed and said "Can we go to the town, Grandpa?" Remembering her manners, she added "Can we, please?" How could Denis refuse a charming invitation like that from one so full of life?

"Of course, my sweet-singing Maisie-bird," he said. "We'll have some breakfast and go this morning, shall we?" He knew that his daughter Susannah needed to get off to work soon and he didn't want to hold her up. "You leave old Grandpa to get dressed and I'll be down in a minute. Please ask Mummy to put the kettle on."

***

The previous day, Denis prepared carefully for the 250 mile drive he was about to undertake. Living so far from his daughter was a problem. Almost as soon as he had adjusted to living without her mother – Amelia had died of cancer a little over two years ago – Susannah, their only child, had been widowed. She and her late husband Patrick had (voluntarily and apparently cheerfully) spent several weekends every year with Denis and Amelia and they had been very kind to him after her death.

Denis missed the quiet, companionable relationship he and Amelia had enjoyed. He had taken some tentative steps to find another partner but internet dating and the terror of speed dating scared him – he would prefer to meet someone in a natural and spontaneous way. But what opportunities existed? Bridge clubs? He didn't play. Ditto squash and chess. Acting? Hardly! A writing group? Maybe, but he'd never put pen to paper . . .

He had also found it hard to work out the roles he and his daughter should play in each other's lives in future. Denis had done everything he could to support Susannah after her husband's tragic death of a heart attack last spring. He had stayed with her and Maisie until Susannah went back to work part-time at the start of the autumn term, at which point she had accepted Denis's offer to child-mind during the week-long school holiday.

But – and it was a big 'but' – would Susannah find Denis's desire to move closer to what remained of his family too intrusive? He had felt unable to obtain the answer to that question during their time together after Patrick's death and the subject was not one he had been prepared to broach on the phone since then. He needed to see Susannah's face as she considered her response. He had resolved to tackle the issue during this visit.

On the journey, Denis's thoughts had turned to the beautiful Maisie. He adored her and was thrilled when Susannah accepted his offer to look after her whenever she needed his help. But, while they lived so far apart, he would never be able to undertake the role of 'childcare assistant' spontaneously. He had to allow an extra day for the journey each side of the time they needed him.

However much effort it took, it was worthwhile! At seven, Maisie was as inquisitive as a puppy and as absorbent as a sponge, bouncing from experience to experience while readily and thoroughly soaking up knowledge. She asked questions all the time and Denis loved to help her to find the answers. If he didn't know they would find out together, using the computer or visiting the library, and sometimes they went on expeditions to solve the puzzles. One of Denis's favourites had answered the question 'Where do birds sleep at night?' And they went on what Denis still thought of as 'nature walks' together, spotting and identifying birds, trees, flowers, fungi and fruit. Sometime they would bring things home – a dead beetle, a fallen leaf and once, to Maisie's great delight, the soft newly-shed skin of a grass snake.

Susannah worked part-time in a supermarket and had to pay for childcare during the school holidays. Even with subsidised rates, Denis knew it was expensive. If he lived nearer he could help out, taking Maisie to and from school and looking after her in the holidays. That would free Susannah to work longer hours.

Despite the joyful prospect of living nearer his daughter and granddaughter, Denis was racked with guilt when he admitted his real motive for moving. He wanted to know that he could rely on Susannah's help if he got frail when he got a lot older. He didn't want to admit to that as his entire motivation and he'd be happier if Susannah saw it simply as an offer of help with Maisie. He felt certain she would welcome that, but would she also see through it?

***

That same morning, while Denis struggled with his conscience, Maisie had simply bounced up and down with joy singing, "Grandpa's coming, Grandpa's coming" when she heard her mother talking to him on the phone. "When will he be here?" she asked and was thrown into a frenzy of activity when she found out he'd arrive later that day. She made a display of the interesting things she had gathered since his last visit. There was a tiny fluffy feather that she'd found in the garden, an acorn which had fallen from the neighbour's tree and a dead butterfly she had found in the garage. Grandpa would know what it was called – mummy didn't.

Shaking her golden curls into a waterfall of light, Maisie asked her mother if they could make a cake for Grandpa. "Why don't you and Grandpa make one together tomorrow?" suggested her exhausted mother. The thought of finding flour and eggs and clearing up the mess afterwards was just too much.

But Maisie's mind was racing and she wasn't really listening. "Can we go to the shops when Grandpa gets here?" she asked, standing on her head on the sofa. Susannah was trying to explain that Grandpa would be tired after the drive and that he wouldn't want to go out until tomorrow when, without waiting to hear her mother's answer, Maisie said, "I'll get my homework to show Grandpa" and dashed up the stairs to find her 'news' book.

Mummy was shouting something up the stairs. Maisie could hear her voice but not the words so she bounced and slid and hopped down the stairs, shouting, "I'm coming." When she got to the kitchen, she was pleased to find out that it was lunchtime. Grandpa was coming after lunch and, if she ate quickly, he'd be here sooner!

***

Maisie's joyful cry of "Grandpa's getting up and we're going to the shops" preceded him down the stairs by a good five minutes. Susannah had her coat on and was ready to leave when he walked into the kitchen.

"Did you sleep well?" she asked, as she poured boiling water on the instant coffee and milk she had mixed in a mug as soon as Maisie returned to the kitchen. "Sorry, but I have to be off soon. Will you be okay? There's loads of food in the fridge: it's mostly expired stuff I got from work but it'll be okay today. You can help yourself to cash from the pot if you need spending money for Maisie. I don't want you spoiling her, mind. No ice cream or sweets if she says she's hungry. There's plenty of fruit and vegetables for her snacks. No cakes and biscuits either – think of her teeth, if nothing else."

Feeling himself thoroughly scolded by his own daughter, Denis sat at the kitchen table while Maisie danced around him. "Has she eaten?" he asked, but his daughter had already left. "Have you had your breakfast?" he asked Maisie, remembering from his last visit that she would ask him for an exotically-named cereal. At least his daughter's access to out-of-date and discounted food meant she could make sure Maisie ate well and, to her credit, the child devoured everything you put in front of her. Denis wasn't worried about how he would feed her: he was more worried about how to stop her eating!

As soon as breakfast was over Maisie invited Denis to inspect her exhibition. She read aloud the latest entry in her homework book and Denis was delighted to hear that it was about how much she had been looking forward to his visit.

He gave his bright and happy granddaughter a big hug and told her how much he loved her. "Thank you Grandpa," said Maisie, giving him a kiss. "Urgh, bristles," she added, running away into the hall. "I'll get my coat."

They set off for the library a little after ten. Denis carried a shopping bag with Maisie's library books and Maisie skipped along beside him, bouncing her pink umbrella on the pavement with every step. "Maisie, if we go to the coffee shop what would you like to drink?" Denis asked. He didn't have a clue what her current favourite might be – her preferences in all things changed so quickly that he couldn't keep up.

"My favourite is raspberry and white chocolate creamy cooler," said Maisie. Her big blue eyes looked up at him hopefully. "It's delicious and creamy and chocolatey. Mummy likes it too and she let me have one as a special treat last time we went to *Cost Of*."

Denis was puzzled. Where was that? "*Cost Of*, Maisie, I don't think I know that shop? Is it in town?"

Maisie looked equally puzzled as she answered, "It's near the library. Mummy says it's a chain. What's that mean? Isn't this a chain?" she asked, holding up the necklace dangling over her fleecy jumper. "How can a coffee shop be like this?"

"Oh my love," laughed Denis. "You say the funniest things. That coffee shop is called Costa and there are lots of them – that's why it's called a chain."

"*Cost Of*, that's what I said," protested Maisie. "Where will we go today? *Cost Of* or somewhere else?"

Denis enjoyed the ambience of *Costa* but he also loved independent coffee shops for the individuality of their owners. He decided they would go to the independent one today. *Cost Of* could wait until another day.

After visiting the library they made their way to the coffee shop. Naturally, it didn't sell raspberry and white chocolate creamy coolers but, after an initial discussion, Maisie agreed to try a banana and strawberry smoothie. As they sat on the comfortably-padded chairs, waiting for their drinks, they looked at the foreign-language newspapers available for patrons. They were laughing at a picture of a squirrel looking in a mirror when someone nearby dropped a cup: the noise made them both jump. They made a game of trying to work out what the stories were about from the photographs illustrating them. At one point Maisie said, "That photo, the one of a woman holding a mobile, that's my Aunty Tracy." Denis was intrigued to hear Maisie mention Patrick's sister. He knew that there had been some difficulty between Susannah, Patrick and Tracy ever since Maisie was born. He had last seen the rather gorgeous Tracy at Patrick's funeral when he had taken both her hands in his to express his condolences. Despite the occasion he found himself attracted to Tracy: he had secretly hoped that the tragedy of Patrick's premature death could heal the rift between his daughter and her sister-in-law but, as far as he knew, things were still difficult between them.

Their drinks arrived. "Try my drink, Grandpa, and I'll try your sprezzo," insisted Maisie. Even without added sugar the smoothie tasted incredibly sweet after the bitter espresso.

Naturally Denis wasn't going to let Maisie taste his drink but, when her smoothie was all gone, he offered her his water. "You can drink as much as you like, Maisie." She finished the glass then, moments later, she started wriggling and said she needed a wee. Looking around, Denis spotted a sign with male and female characters and a wheelchair. What to do? He didn't fancy taking Maisie into the gents' and he didn't feel comfortable going into the ladies' with her. Should he use the disabled facilities as they were unisex?

This was a new conundrum for him – Susannah, Patrick or Amelia had always taken Maisie to the lavatory in the past – and he was struggling to solve the problem as they made their way to the back of the coffee shop. The anxiety he felt must have showed on his face because he heard a woman's voice as she approached them from behind. "Would you like me to take . . . her to the loo?" she said as Maisie hopped from foot to foot in desperation, pulling Denis towards the lavatory and away from the woman. As he looked down at the child, Denis empathised with her and made an instantaneous decision.

"Thank you," he answered. "I was just wondering how to go about it! I'll wait here for you." He turned to look at the woman, seeing only her back as she passed him and took Maisie's hand. The little girl hurriedly dragged her helper towards the lavatory. Denis could see the door of the ladies' from where he stood and, as it closed behind the two of them, he remembered hearing the slight hesitation as the woman spoke. He thought there was something familiar about her voice: was that possible? Who was she? Denis realised that he couldn't even describe her face – all his attention had been on the child and he hadn't looked at the woman. Did she represent a threat to Maisie? How could he have been so naive? Should he try to enter the cubicle, despite the gender symbol on the door?

With all these thoughts – and many more, unspeakably awful, ones – crowding his mind, Denis approached the door and knocked loudly. He said, clearly enough for the other customers to hear, "Is everything all right in there? Is my granddaughter okay?"

Maisie's muffled, cheery voice said, "Hello, Grandpa."

An adult female voice called out, "We'll be with you in a minute," then, more quietly, "no, don't open the door yet, Maisie."

Denis paced up and down the corridor outside the lavatory. How long did it take a seven-year-old to empty her tiny bladder? Not this long, surely. And the woman's words suggested that Maisie wasn't sitting on the lavatory. What was going on in there? How did the woman know Maisie's name? Had the naive child told the stranger, or did the woman know her? He was about to knock again when the door opened and Maisie skipped out, smiling broadly. "Grandpa – look, it's Aunty Tracy," she said. "She took a picture of me in the toilet."

In his anxiety Denis didn't pay any attention to Maisie's second sentence. "I'm sorry," he said to Tracy. "I didn't recognise you. We haven't met very often since Susannah and Patrick's wedding, have we, and . . . " He was about to say that he was sorry he hadn't had the chance to speak to her for longer at the funeral when he remembered the difficulty between her and Susannah. "I was heartbroken by your brother's death. Such a lovely man. Susannah went back to work recently and this is half-term week so Maisie has to put up with me looking after her."

"I thought I recognised you when I walked in but I didn't like to interrupt." Tracy's voice was concerned and kind. "I hardly see young Maisie these days, since . . . Well, for a while. It's a lovely coincidence that you chose to come in here today."

Looking down at Maisie, Denis saw her gazing up at them and, when she spoke, it was with the directness that only a child can get away with. "Can Aunty Tracy come and help us make the cake this afternoon, Grandpa? Please say you'll come, Aunty Tracy. It's going to be a big round cake with bananas in it, isn't it Grandpa? You can take a picture of that too – look, Grandpa. Tracy's phone takes pictures."

Pictures? Hadn't Maisie said something about a picture in the toilet? What kind of picture was that? "Can I see the photo you took

80

of Maisie?" he stammered, embarrassed that his mind was capable of such unpleasant thoughts. Tracy handed over her phone but Denis was baffled by its plain glass screen. She ran her finger across it and there appeared an image of Maisie standing behind the closed lavatory door, arms raised like a ballet dancer and with a cheeky grin on her face.

Denis blushed as he said, "That's lovely. Can you send it to me by email?" When Tracy nodded he dictated his address. "Thank you," he said as Tracy deftly tapped the details into her phone.

"There: you should be able to see it next time you check your email," she said. Turning to the little girl twirling around her legs she said, "I'd love to make a cake with you, Maisie, but I have lots of things to do this afternoon. Another day perhaps. Please ask your mummy to ring me."

Denis was disappointed that Tracy appeared to be about to leave. "Can you spare the time to join us for an early lunch?" he asked. "They do sandwiches and soup here – should be something for Maisie." Tracy's smile and nod warmed and soothed Denis's trembling heart.

Their conversation over lunch was open and friendly, with Tracy enquiring after Denis's health. She even suggested that it was a shame he lived so far away, words which made him hope that she might be interested in him romantically. 'Don't be such a fool,' he thought when he looked in the mirror in the gents' toilet a few minutes later. 'She's beautiful and young – what would she see in you?'

But when Tracy kissed and hugged them both before she left the coffee shop those feelings were revived in him. Maisie promised to tell her mummy that they had met Aunty Tracy.

Denis hoped that he would be able to see Tracy again, but just the two of them this time. 'Yes,' thought Denis as he and Maisie kicked up the fallen leaves as they walked home. 'I'd really like to see Tracy on her own . . . ' Maybe he'd found another reason to move home, a more honest one, and maybe he had solved the long-term care problem too!

CAPPUCCINO

by Liz Losty

KATE arrived in town and prayed for a parking space on the High Street so she wouldn't have far to walk to the coffee shop. She pounced, with brake lights and indicator flashing, as she saw a black sports car pulling out from a space. She parked then turned off the engine and sat quietly for a moment, collecting her thoughts, before giving herself a shake and getting out of the car. She walked quickly towards the coffee shop to compensate for her lateness. Helen's sympathy would soon evaporate if she was kept waiting.

The coffee shop was busy when Kate arrived. As she scanned the faces looking for Helen, she saw an old friend, Miriam, sitting by herself at a table so she fixed a smile to her face and walked over to say hello. They had been on a cookery course together. Miriam had always liked evening classes, and learning to cook was a hobby her husband had quietly encouraged. Kate's husband had encouraged her night classes too, only now Kate realised how he had played her so that he had free evenings to wine and dine Emma. She decided not to mention the divorce to Miriam.

Miriam smiled thinly as Kate walked over, and put her hand on the spare chair. "I hope you don't mind, Kate, but I'm meeting someone. A work meeting. Otherwise I would invite you to join me."

"Oh I'm meeting someone too. I just wanted to say hello. Don't worry, I won't keep you." Kate turned away without a smile or goodbye. She knew she had sounded brittle, but she was a little hurt by the obvious rebuff.

She used to get on with Miriam like a house on fire but today it was as if she was the last person Miriam wanted to see. Why on earth would she be like that? What had Kate done to upset her? Maybe she had heard about the divorce and didn't want to get dragged into the role of counsellor? With bruised feelings, Kate moved to the counter and ordered her skinny cappuccino and one for Helen so she wouldn't have to queue when she arrived. Then, spotting a table by the window, Kate carried the tray over and sat down. She felt a bit affronted that, for the first time, she was waiting for Helen rather than the other way round and felt slightly self-conscious sitting by herself. She sat with her back to Miriam so that she didn't seem needy or nosy.

She watched an older man and a little girl chatter and laugh at a nearby table and, for once in her life, wished herself older. She wondered at the joy she would gain from taking Jamie's children out to a coffee shop for treats and cakes, and thought wistfully how it would feel to be loved and needed as a grandmother and to have a baby around to love and fuss over. Was that all there was left to look forward to? She still wanted to think of herself as a well groomed, attractive and sophisticated lady. Surely she should not wish her life away? She took such a pride in her appearance – part of the reason she was running late today was the indecision over what to wear.

Kate had opened the wardrobe doors in her bedroom that morning with a dramatic flourish, and took her time selecting and rejecting outfits before settling on the cream jacket to complement the silk blouse and navy wool trousers. It was only when she was fully dressed and already running late that she realised, with a tut of annoyance, there was a stain on the jacket pocket. She hoped no-one would notice and think that she had gone to seed.

She liked to appear groomed and well-dressed but her weakness now was that she only saw herself through the eyes of others and found it harder than ever to maintain the standard she had set for herself. Money was short, of course, and that was one of her constant worries. Even the dry cleaning bills seemed extortionately expensive now, another reminder of the pittance Andrew had settled on her in the divorce.

It was always Kate's habit to check herself for the final time in the mirror, then spritz her favourite perfume around her neck and wrists.

She grabbed her handbag and headed downstairs to the front door. Opening it, she hesitated. Kate had started to develop other habits, one of which was forgetfulness. She started rummaging in her handbag and realised she had left her mobile phone on the kitchen counter, still charging. She grabbed it then double-checked that the back door was locked, that she had her keys and purse before finally leaving the house.

In the 'old days' as she referred to them, she would have sauntered out of the house with hardly a care. But now that Andrew was gone, and she was living by herself for the first time in thirty years, she found she was double-checking everything and always forgetting something.

Her mind drifted while she waited for Helen. She thought of all the events over recent months and all of the upheaval and unhappiness, before her inner voice settled once again on the path of self-criticism and how badly she felt she was coping. She thought of the lost car keys and the unlocked doors. At first she was convinced that it was the anti-depressants making her forgetful, then she thought it might be the anti-anxiety remedy a friend had recommended.

Kate had come to the conclusion that it was just her, the fear she felt at being alone and having to start all over again at her age.

She had once confided to Helen that she would have been happier if Andrew had died, maybe in a car crash or from a sudden heart attack. If only he had been taken from her in that way, not wanting to go, but taken from her nonetheless. Helen had looked at her in shock when she said it. Her expression said much more than her words. "Oh Kate, don't say that, don't wish him dead. You are a kinder soul than that, a much better person."

Kate had stared at Helen as she realised what her friend meant. It was then she felt the tears coming, her shame and downfall complete. Grasping the tissues Helen offered her and attempting to dry her tears, she tried to explain what drove such wicked thoughts.

"It was the rejection, that's what I couldn't bear. Don't you see Helen? If he had died, that would have meant he had been taken away from me. But that's not what happened. He chose someone else, he left me. He had a choice and he left me."

Then she had cried like a child, her shoulders racking and shaking, her face buried in the rags of wet tissues. Helen could only hold her, hug her, reassure her that the pain would pass and that she was too good for Andrew, he was a fool. All the usual weak platitudes.

It was such a cliché, the middle-aged man leaving his wife for his secretary who was twenty years younger. Everyone else at the office had known about the affair for months. It was the final disgrace, the fact that everyone knew but no-one said anything. Then the pity in their eyes on that day when Kate walked into the office and saw Emma sitting on Andrew's desk. They were holding hands. It was such a simple act to witness and yet their easiness with each other, the proximity of her body to his, his eyes on her, told of such intimacy.

It had been her only clue, but Kate had stopped still and looked at them in surprise before they noticed her. Andrew looked up and whispered something to Emma, who turned to look at Kate and back at Andrew before casually sliding off his desk and walking slowly, sexily, defiantly back to her own desk nearby.

Kate felt dizzy, out of step. She faltered and looked around the office, trying to collect herself. She noticed two or three members of the architectural team looking at her then quickly looking away in embarrassment. The sudden silence in the office spoke volumes. That's when she knew for sure.

Kate had walked over to Andrew's desk. "Andrew . . . ?" but she couldn't say any more. He had whisked her into a side office before she caused a scene and told her not to say anything, then sent her home in a cab saying he would be home shortly. She did as she was told; silent, compliant, stunned.

She waited until he arrived home, and that was when he told her, packed a bag and left. "I am in love with her, Kate, you have got to understand that. We both feel terrible about how this has happened. Emma has been in tears every time we've talked about it, you have no idea how much all of this has upset her."

"Oh, poor Andrew." Kate spat the words out. "And poor Emma. To think she has been upset. How awful for that self-centred, cunning little cow. All the times I have left messages for you with her, chatted to her on the phone, bought her thank-you presents…" It was the irony of that last thought that set Kate off. She had started laughing then, huge roaring laughs, hysterical whoops that gave vent to the depth of emotion she felt and which, inevitably, gave way to sobbing tears. But Andrew had already left before the tears came.

There had been no further discussion, no weekly sessions with a marriage counsellor, no trial separation, no mediation. Andrew had planned his escape route long ago and wanted a quick divorce so he could move on. Only his ex-wife and family were left behind.

Jamie had taken the news almost as badly as Kate. He promised his mother he had known nothing of the affair, despite regularly popping into his dad's office for advice or to report on his latest job interview. He got angry every time the subject of Emma came up, and shouted at his mother to stop talking about her. If she didn't, he stormed out of the room.

His temper could be frightening and, at nineteen years of age, he towered over Kate so she quickly let the subject of Emma drop for fear of his temper and, worse, her fear of driving him away too. She had lost one man in her life: she didn't want to risk losing another. She reasoned that Jamie's anger was to be expected. He was an only child and close to both his parents, so of course he was devastated by their divorce.

While Kate had plenty of venom for Emma, she had decided from the beginning never to speak ill of Andrew in front of Jamie. Not because she loved Andrew any longer, but because she loved Jamie so much she didn't want to make him any unhappier or angrier than he already was. In some ways she cursed herself for encouraging him to take a year out before he went to university. His plan had been to work for six months then travel for six months before embarking on his degree. He had been living at home when Kate had discovered Andrew's affair and had been there to witness the fall out, the move out and the quick divorce which Andrew readily agreed to on the grounds of his adultery. Jamie had seen and heard too much already.

Kate's thoughts always moved in this cyclical pattern, from where she was now, through where she had been, to what she had lost and what would she do. She couldn't stop it and yet knew how damaging it was. She stared at the cappuccino she had bought Helen. It now looked flat and tepid. It had been left too long, and was probably undrinkable. Where was Helen?

***

As Helen walked towards the coffee shop she could see Kate through the window, sitting by herself with a sad expression on her face. Helen steeled herself. She hated to be the bearer of bad news, but she knew Andrew was a coward. Helen had only found out because she saw them looking at cots and prams in the nursery department, Emma flushed with excitement and Andrew just looking flushed. Helen had slipped away before Andrew saw her. Kate had never mentioned it so Helen realised she didn't know. Helen decided her approach on breaking the news to Kate would be along the lines of 'Poor Andrew!' and 'Can you imagine going through all that again at his age?' Kate would soon get her revenge once she got over the shock.

Helen opened the door and smiled as Kate looked up and pointed at the cappuccino she had already bought Helen. The queue for drinks was so long that Helen felt particularly grateful to have one waiting for her. After initial comments about the parking problems in the town, and how busy it was today, Helen decided to tear the plaster off. "Kate, I just wanted to let you know. I saw Emma and Andrew shopping the other day."

"Oh, yes? Well he's always happy to spend money on her," muttered Kate.

"Well, the thing is, and I am not saying this to upset you . . . " Helen hesitated, wondering if there was any way to soften the blow. Kate looked up from her coffee cup, a wary expression on her face. She was giving Helen her full attention now.

"Kate, the thing is, they were shopping for prams and a cot, and by the look of Emma I would say she is six or seven months gone. I'm sorry to be the bearer of upsetting news but I thought you should know."

Kate's half-empty cup clattered to the floor and smashed. The little girl sitting nearby with the older man, her grandfather perhaps, jumped at the sound. A woman came from behind the counter, picked up the broken cup and wiped away the spilt coffee with a cloth.

Kate's mind replayed Helen's words again and again as she raced through all the possible implications of this bombshell. "Andrew is such a fool. What a stupid old fool! And poor Jamie, this is going to kill him! Can you imagine? He has always been our only child, and now this! I need to tell him. No doubt Andrew will have avoided breaking this news to him. He always avoids all the difficult conversations, he is so damned weak." Kate had already pulled her mobile phone out of her handbag and was calling Jamie. She made herself sound bright and breezy when he answered, and suggested they meet for a coffee later that day since she was in town shopping. Once the meeting time was agreed she hung up and looked at Helen. The smiling mask fell from her face and she looked broken.

"Why do I feel that I am the only one who cares about Jamie's feelings?" she asked Helen. "Why am I the only one who is the adult here? A baby, for God's sake, he's having a baby, at his age? Just when I thought it couldn't get any worse!"

She paused again, thinking of the baby she and Andrew had loved so much, her mind going back to when Jamie was born. The joy, the surge and depth of such powerful maternal love, the sleepless nights, the teething, the exhaustion, the constant worry, the weaning, the night feeds.

She looked at Helen. "Gosh, when I really think about it, I almost feel sorry for Andrew."

Her mind started working again as she did the maths. "Imagine being a father again at the age of fifty-five! When he is seventy, it will still be a child. In fact, it will be a fifteen-year-old teenager with all the storms that brings! As for Emma, let's see how she copes with a new baby, a flabby tummy, sleepless nights and smelling of sick. There will be a lot less time and money to spend on designer clothes, or at the hairdressers getting her fake nails and her fake tan done, she's about to hit reality!"

Kate and Helen looked at each other, their expressions mirroring each other from horror to mirth as they both burst into laughter.

"Poor Andrew," Kate said. And this time she genuinely meant it. And for the first time since her heart had been broken, she felt a growing sense of freedom.

CHAI LATTE

by Richard Hopgood

SHE was seated by a window when he arrived, a diminutive figure half hidden by a copy of the *Financial Times* she held aloft to catch the light. He knew it was her by the Victorian ankle boots she always wore at this time of year. 'A bit young,' he thought, but like most things she carried it off.

He braced himself for the theatrical "Darling!" with which she usually greeted him outside the boardroom, but she merely lowered the paper and smiled. He sat down opposite her with his espresso and saw with surprise that she had a large mug of chai latte. "You won't get much caffeine from that, Miriam," he said, arching his eyebrows quizzically.

"Mimi needs sweetness and warmth this morning," she murmured, and lent over to peck him on the cheek.

Miriam was in her early sixties. Nobody was sure of her exact age, which had become vaguer with the passing of the years, but it would have been more than foolhardy to ask. They had both been in the advertising business since the 1970s, initially on the same account at J Walter Thompson then going their separate ways for smaller and more agile outfits. She had eventually set up her own company and, for a period, it looked as if she would become an industry titan. But arguments over bonuses had led to defections, and she had eventually left and lain low for a while. Some people thought she had suffered a nervous breakdown. Then they had both joined Z, she in charge of marketing, he on the creative side. Now he was the Chairman and she was his deputy. They made a formidable duo.

As he sipped his coffee, Miriam continued to read the paper. He felt, rather than saw, her glancing at him every so often from the half-moon glasses which she wore halfway down her nose. His quick eye took in the surroundings – the mix of old armchairs and kitchen tables, the books in alcoves, the Fair Trade adverts.

"Ethical chic," he muttered.

"Don't be such a snob, Geoff, it's a good little business. Look at all the young mums. Right up their street . . . "

He did not respond. She had obviously not asked him to meet her here for a chat about coffee shops. He assumed it was for some office politicking in advance of next Thursday's board meeting, when battle was to be rejoined between the 'steady-as-she-goes' and the 'grow-or-die' factions. He and Miriam had been around the block often enough to know that both were right at different times, but never all the time. That was the trouble. They had converted business strategy into philosophies. But so long as he and Miriam saw eye to eye, they could keep their fractious colleagues under control and the owners content. And up to now they always had.

After some minutes, Miriam folded the paper and placed it on the table. He looked at her fine features – the thin lips, the mournful Jewish eyes with their wells of ancient sadness – and felt a wave of fondness. She still retained her mystique.

He expected her to say something. She didn't, but just looked at him with a half smile. The silence discomforted him. "How's Harry?" he asked, breaking the ice.

"Oh, he's fine. At home, supervising some men putting in a new Aga. They don't need supervising and he knows nothing about Agas, but you know what he's like. He has to pretend he's in charge." She chuckled. She had been married to Harry for fifteen years after a turbulent love life and two divorces, and had found contentment. They were inseparable.

"And Julian?" Her son, an only child, was in his twenties and trying to get into the film industry.

"Struggling. But he's like his father, he never gives up. He's been in New York for the last week. We spoke last night . . . " She did not go on, which was unusual. She liked nothing better than talking about

Julian, especially to anybody who could help him.

"All ready for the board meeting? I'm seeing Simon later today, just to make sure he's on side." Simon was their main liaison with the owner.

"Good," she said, without enthusiasm. "I'm sure he'll be happy with our line."

"Growth with care, that's their mantra. No sudden surges. Wait until the market settles down and strengthens. Anyway, you know all the arguments . . . "

"I do indeed, darling, but that's not why I asked to meet you." She fell quiet again. He finished his espresso and signalled for a refill. He wanted to be at his sharpest for the meeting with Simon.

As he tore the top off a thin sleeve of sugar and poured it into his fresh espresso he looked at her. Miriam was usually the life and soul of the party, with a constant stream of invective and repartee which held you through her sheer energy and chutzpah. It was as if she was walking a tightrope of words across an abyss of silence and could not pause for breath until she reached the other side. It enabled her to dominate meetings. In her early days in what had been an almost entirely male industry, men had usually been too polite to interrupt. If they became hostile, she had turned on her charm and sexuality like a search light, and more often than not it worked. She could over-dramatise to the point of melodrama and, at these moments, Geoff sensed her brittleness and rode to her rescue. But today she seemed curiously flat.

"What it is Miriam?" he asked, in a lowered tone. "You're getting me worried."

"Don't worry, it'll be alright, you'll be alright, I promise," she responded, squeezing his hand.

"But what is it?"

"It? Well, that's more difficult. I call it my 'uninvited guest' who needs to be cajoled and bribed and if necessary threatened to leave but who, for the time being, I have to treat as a friend."

He looked at her, puzzled. She lifted her mug and drained her chai latte. An arch of white froth hung on her lower lip. She folded a serviette and dabbed under her nose. Her eyes looked moist.

"And who is the uninvited guest? Another member of the board?" he asked, wondering whether she was asking him to get rid of somebody the private equity company had just put on.

"Oh, would that it were!" She giggled childishly.

"Well, Miriam, put me out of my misery. Who is it?" He spoke louder than he intended.

She pulled her jacket tight around herself, as if huddling inside it. "Do I seem different?" she asked, in a pouting little girl's voice.

"Yes," he said.

"Well, I've had some bad news." She went quiet, then sobbed. "I've got breast cancer."

He gasped, genuinely shocked. "Are you sure?" he blurted out.

"I had a scan last week. It's been there a while, and it might already have spread." By now she had regained control of herself, and her voice was firm and unpitying.

"But they can treat it, right, and get rid of it?"

"It's not that simple. I'm afraid it's rather taken hold." She raised her eyes and looked at him squarely. "I may not have terribly long."

He moved his chair closer to her and put an arm round her. "We can't afford to lose you Miriam. You've got to come through this . . . " he muttered, desperately trying to find some words of encouragement which did not sound trite.

"Well, Geoff, I'll do my very, very best, darling, but I'm trying to tell you . . . "

Her emotions overcame her and she covered her face with her tiny gloved hands, weeping silently.

As she did so, he was already wondering who should take her place as Vice Chair. He would have to move quickly to put in somebody he could rely on before the factions tried to organise their own candidates.

"Can I tell Simon? If you need some time away, we need to appoint an Acting Vice Chair quickly, before things get messy . . . "

"Yes, I know, I know. I've thought about it, and I think Kenneth is your man."

He nodded, doubtfully. Ken was not altogether reliable. "Will you be coming to the board meeting? I'll have to tell them beforehand, if we're going to propose a replacement . . . "

His voice tailed off. He sounded callous. He did not mean to. He squeezed her arm. "Don't do that, you'll make me cry again," she said miserably. She looked at him with a look almost of love, and he felt his own eyes moisten.

"Don't be silly, darling, it may just be a false alarm. You know how gloomy these consultants can be. Can't bear to be wrong in case you sue them. Which, by God, I would if I had to . . . " She straightened her hair, unclipped her bag, and applied some fresh lipstick. "Time to face the world – and Harry – again. How do I look?"

"Wonderful," he murmured.

She rose, kissed him, gathered up the café's FT and put it under her arm. "I'll see you on Monday, sweetie. You can tell the board then." She hesitated, then lifted her head and looked him in the eye. "But make sure it's only an acting appointment. If there's a snowball's chance in hell of returning, I damn well will."

She laughed, ruffled his hair with her hand, and walked briskly to the exit, waving as she departed. He watched her walk to the little sports car, parked on a yellow line, and get in.

He stirred the remains of his espresso and spooned it into his mouth. It was cold. He shuddered with distaste, then wondered what he should say to Simon. Ken really would not do, even as a stand-in.

ICED COFFEE

by Debbie Hunter

THE novel taste of the coffee matches the novel feeling of confidence. She feels as if she has stepped out of an old shy skin and a new confident person has emerged – an attractive person, she hopes, ready to take on relationships. She's even dressed differently today, abandoning her usual choice of black and beige. Her pink top has been retrieved from where she threw it to the back of her cupboard. 'Cotton Candy,' it said on the label. She hasn't worn it since the time her father had told her she'd stand out like a sore thumb in it. Today she doesn't care. Today she is reckless.

The drink has taken her by surprise, this strange sensation of drinking freezing liquid. She hadn't expected it to taste as cold. Stop being stupid, she thinks to herself, what else would you expect from an iced coffee with chinking ice cubes and condensation forming on the glass? She thinks iced coffee is a taste oxymoron. Coffee should be hot, tantalising and stimulating. That it could also be freezing, tantalising and stimulating is exhilarating. She tells herself that drinking it will make her bold and adventurous.

Once more she glances expectantly at the door and then looks around at the occupants of the neighbouring tables. They are all involved in their own little worlds. Mothers attending to their unruly children. A man at the next table saying comforting words to his sad companion, a woman who looks older than him, and stroking her arm.

Nobody is taking any notice of her, sitting at a table for two with the significant empty chair. She takes the guide book out of her bag and pages through it, feigning intense interest although she knows the contents by heart. She'd spent most of the night researching her home town. She wishes she'd brought a magazine. She hadn't been expecting to sit here for so long.

She takes another sip of the coffee through the straw, her mouth and throat becoming accustomed to the cold. She likes the taste of the sweet icy creaminess combined with the coffee bitterness. At first she had wanted to gulp it down quickly, she didn't feel it was a drink to be daintily sipped. She is eager to relish the taste but is reluctant to finish it. She notices the top of the straw stained with lipstick. 'Pink Fizz' is not a colour she usually wears.

Her fingers play with a strand of hair hanging down her face. She's not used to it being loose. She feels self-conscious, and stops.

She looks at her watch. Usually she would be heading back to work at this time. She thinks back to yesterday when she was in the coffee shop during her lunch hour ignorant of what lay in store for her. For once she'd been in the right place at the right time.

It had been busy in the coffee shop yesterday. Customers standing around, trying not to look at those sitting at tables but silently willing them to finish their drinks and go. She'd been lucky to find a table. She'd looked up when she heard the voice, an accent divulging a stranger.

"OK if I sit here?" The first thing she'd noticed was the way his dark hair framed his rounded face. He obviously wasn't local; locals knew the unspoken etiquette of respecting a private space at a table. They knew strangers didn't share.

He hadn't waited for an answer before sitting down at the chair facing her and unloading his tray. His backpack knocked against her handbag as he dropped it on the floor. She watched him as he set down the tall frosty glass containing the light brown milky liquid topped with cream. He bit hungrily into a chocolate muffin. Discarding the straw he took long gulps of the iced coffee, the layers blending in the glass as he drank. She realised she was staring at him and quickly averted her eyes back to the book she had been reading.

"Wow! That stuff's really good," she heard him say. "Haven't tasted anything so good since I left home."

She watched as he wiped his mouth with his sleeve, leaving a small trail of cream on his unshaven face. She knew she should have been repelled but strangely she was intrigued by his lack of manners. She thought his accent was American, or maybe Canadian. Casualness was apparent throughout his whole being, the slightly-too-long hair, the faded suede jacket partially covering the logo on the washed-out T shirt. The woollen scarf draped round his neck seemed at odds with the rest of his clothing.

She tried to guess his age. He looked out of place among the conservatively dressed coffee shop customers.

"Do you live in this town?" She jumped. She hadn't expected him to speak to her.

"Yes," she answered, "I do."

"Lived here long?"

"All my life."

"Wow – kinda boring."

She supposed it was, but then the whole of her life was boring. She'd reached the age of twenty-four without managing to do anything of interest. She had done well enough at school, had achieved average marks at university. She regretted not leaving home as most of her friends had done. Her parents had pleaded financial difficulties so she had compliantly attended the local university. Her parents, elderly compared to those of her peers, dissuaded her from most things. Even her looks and her clothes were boring; brown hair, brown eyes, beige clothes. And that was why she'd never had a boyfriend. "Plenty of time for those when you're older," her mother always said. How much older would she have to be?

"Do you work here in this town too?"

"Yes."

"What do you do?"

"I work for the council – administrative assistant."

Why had she told him she was an assistant? Why did she even mention the council? She could have made up something glamorous. She could have said she was in PR or marketing. PR sounded far more interesting than administration. Why was she even talking to him?

"I guess you know this place well. I just got here. Didn't really mean to come here but got on the wrong train." He gave a laugh as he said this and she noticed his straight white teeth, the way the tanned skin around his eyes crinkled as he smiled. She thought his name would be Kurt, or Buzz or Chad. "But I thought that since I was here I might as well look around. Glad I did. This is the best iced coffee I've had for a while. Guess most places don't know how to make it over here."

She didn't know how to answer, or even if a reply was expected, so she gave a half smile.

"You must be an expert on this place since you've lived here all your life – what's there to do here?"

What was there to do here? She suddenly found herself eager to impress him, wanting to make herself and the town more attractive than it was.

"Well, the old part of town is nice, lots of tourists go there. There's an old church and old pubs. It's been described as quaint."

"Quaint? Don't have much 'quaint' where I come from."

"Where's that?"

"Wadeville North Dakota – ever heard of it?"

"No."

"Neither have most people." He laughed again. "'Bout the most interesting fact about Wadeville is that the ratio of males to females is nearly 50:50 – almost exactly one to one – a woman for every man."

He stretched out the word 'woman' as he looked intently at her, making her feel uncomfortable. Was this flirting? She'd had no experience of flirting so couldn't tell. Discomfort turned to excitement. "Trouble is most of the women are so damn ugly you don't want your one." He laughed at his own humour and took another mouthful of the cold coffee. "Might as well as have a look at 'quaint' while I'm here. Do you know anywhere I could stay tonight? Somewhere cheap?"

She was about to say that she didn't then she remembered that the library had a list of local accommodation. "You can probably get some information at the library. I'm going past there now. It's on my way back to work – would you like me to take you there?" She hoped she didn't sound too eager.

"Sure – that'd be good."

He gulped down the rest of his drink, picked up his backpack and followed her out of the coffee shop. She noticed that he was slightly taller than her, that his shoes and jeans were scruffy, that he was the type of person her father would despise.

She showed him where to find the list of accommodation at the library. She was reluctant to leave him but she had to get back to work. "I've got to go now – hope you find somewhere to stay." He was looking at a brochure showing the local attractions.

"Seems there's quite a lot of quaint here – how about you showing me some of it? Wanna meet up tomorrow?"

His request startled her while the thought of seeing him again unnerved her more. She was annoyed to find herself blushing. "Um . . . Yes . . . OK." Surely she could get some time off work – she'd make some excuse or other.

"How about we meet at the coffee shop tomorrow?" he urged.

"OK, that would be lovely." She wasn't sure what she would tell her boss. Could she invent a dentist appointment? Lies did not come easily to her. "I could get there about one o'clock."

"Great! See you then." He swung his backpack onto his shoulders and waved to her as he left the library. She watched as he walked along the street.

A feeling of pure exhilaration flowed through her as she went back to her desk. It was an emotion new to her. She found it difficult to concentrate on her work. Staring out of the window, she fantasised about her date the next day. She decided it was definitely a date. Where would she take him? What would they talk about?

What would she wear? She'd wear her hair loose, not dragged back in the usual style. She'd discard her glasses in favour of her seldom-used contact lenses. She would get to the coffee shop in plenty of time, she didn't want to waste a minute of his company. She realised she didn't know his name and he didn't know hers. She would be Suzi. 'Susan' discarded with the glasses and the beige. She would drink iced coffee.

***

She looks at her watch again and sighs. The older woman at the next table is saying goodbye to her companion. He looks worried. Many of the tables are now empty. She looks at the door again. Her eyes are beginning to itch. She picks up her bag and takes out her glasses and a plastic container. Turning around so that no-one can see she removes the lenses from her eyes and places them in the small container. She puts it back in her bag and takes out a hairband. The lipstick falls from her bag. She scrapes her hair back and secures it with the band, tightly, no strands escape. She puts on her glasses and looks once more at the door.

Two mouthfuls and the drink is finished. Shivering she puts on the beige cardigan, obliterating the pink top. She stands up and leaves the coffee shop, throwing the lipstick in the bin as she passes.

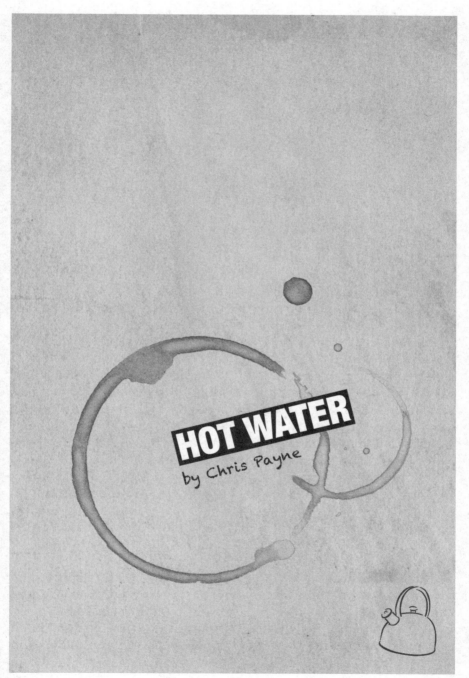

HOT WATER
by Chris Payne

BRYAN jumped down the stairs two at a time and burst into the kitchen. His mother saluted him absently with her cigarette from the kitchen table, but didn't lift her eyes from the newspaper.

"Mum," Bryan said urgently. "Have you seen my bag? The one with all my *Young Enterprise* stuff in it? I had it last night."

His mother looked up and spoke slowly. "Hello, love. What does it look like? You could try looking in the front hall. Danny Powell's died."

Bryan lunged for the hallway. "It's a *Morrison's* bag. It has all my papers in it for the *Young Enterprise* thing. I'm meeting Shona today, remember?" Bryan began rooting violently through the pile of coats and shoes next to the front door. He called back, "Who's Danny Powell?"

"That children's entertainer, had a live rabbit on stage. He's been on the local circuit for years, you went to a party with him once. Shona ate too much ice cream and was sick."

"I remember the rabbit. Here's my bag! Why did you have to move my stuff?"

"Funny you'll be seeing Shona again today after all these years. I wonder if she still loves ice cream?" mused his mother, turning the page of the newspaper.

"Right, I'm off now Mum, got this meeting. I won't be back till late probably. And Mum… how about getting dressed, yeah? It's past lunchtime."

As the slamming door echoed through the house, Joanna Smith rose and crossed to the worktop to re-boil the kettle. 'It must be eight years since Bryan's seen Shona,' she thought. 'Just before they started secondary school.' At one point the two of them had been inseparable.

She remembered his first day at nursery as if it were yesterday. He'd been so shy, never wanting to leave her side and always clutching 'binkit' his comfort blanket. She'd been desperate for him to settle at nursery so that she could get a more regular job. The benefits just weren't stretching far enough. But with Bryan's clinginess and patchy toilet training, she hadn't been sure that the nursery would keep him.

She'd been standing at the front, talking to the lady in charge, with one of Bryan's little arms wrapped firmly around her leg and his other hand clutching binkit. The lady had been looking doubtful and explaining how they couldn't take responsibility for cleaning Bryan up all the time. It was happening too frequently. Joanna had been making promises about Bryan's toilet habits that she knew were out of her power to keep. Suddenly a little voice near her knee had said, 'Will you come and eat the dinner I've made?'

Joanna had looked down to see a yellow-haired little angel holding out a plate of plastic food to Bryan. She'd been about to demur on his behalf and send the girl away, when Bryan had carefully unwrapped his arm from his mother's leg and trotted off after the girl without a backward glance. She and the nursery leader had looked at each other and laughed in astonishment. It was the first time they hadn't had to peel Bryan off Joanna, finger by finger.

The next day Bryan had left his binkit at home, and every day afterwards it was Shona this, Shona that. It didn't change when they moved to the local primary school: when you might have expected that they would split off into boy and girl camps, they'd stayed firm friends.

'Both being Smiths helped a bit, kept them sitting together at school,' Bryan's mum thought idly as she stirred her tea. 'Plus being the only two in the class with single mothers. With them both in breakfast club and after-school club every day while Shirley and I were working, they got thrown together a lot. And every weekend in the park, that little den they had. They'd spend hours in that scrubby patch under the oak tree, with Shona making her meals of leaves and grass, and Bryan building his ant mazes. It's nice that they are meeting again now. I wonder what they'll find to say to each other?' She looked out at the dark and windy afternoon, shivered, and pulled her flowered housecoat tighter. "No harm in a lazy day now and again," she said to herself as she returned to her paper.

***

Bryan shivered at the bus stop, trying to tuck his carrier bag under his jacket against the rain. He jumped back as the bus pulled in, but the splash from the kerbside puddle still soaked the bottom of his jeans. He pulled up the hood of his sweatshirt and kept his gaze fixed on the bus steps to avoid the other passengers' pitying looks.

Inside the bus, the heating system valiantly battled the chill October air and people's damp coats created a steamy fug. Bryan lurched down the central aisle to an empty seat and squeezed past the knees of a plump young woman to claim it. He folded his long frame into the small space with his bag on his lap. He couldn't resist peeping inside again, just to check. There it was in black and white:

John Carpenter School has been paired with Connington House School for Young Enterprise. The leader of Connington House's team is Shona Harris-Smith, whose contact details are attached to this letter. Team leaders from each school should meet before term re-starts to determine the meeting schedule for your combined group. Further resources to assist with this are available on the Young Enterprise website. We wish your team every success!

'So she did change her name,' had been Bryan's first thought when he read the letter. He remembered when she'd told him about the move. As usual they'd been sitting under the blanket he'd rigged into a tent in his room. Shona's mum had just dropped her off and was downstairs having a cup of tea with his mum. Suddenly they heard a great squealing and laughter from Bryan's mum, and her voice came up the stairs. "Time to break out the champagne! Nice one, Shirl!"

"What's that about?" Bryan had asked Shona.

"Mum must've told her our news," Shona had said.

Her mum was getting married again. She'd been a serial dater as long as Bryan had known Shona; he'd lost count of the number of times he'd been round to her house and found a different 'uncle' sitting at the kitchen table. Lately, though, it had mainly been 'Mr Big', as Shona called him because of his flashy car. But married? He almost missed Shona's next statement.

"Mum's already put the house on the market."

"Why is she doing that?"

"Bryan, weren't you listening? We're going to move in with Mr Big. He has this big posh house and I'm going to have this huge bedroom, you wouldn't believe it! There's room for a desk and a couch and a double bed and I get my own TV in my room! And an Xbox! Mr Big says I can have whatever I want in there, and I can decorate it however I want. I'm going to have it pink."

Bryan had gazed at her mutely. Shona hated pink.

Shona had been restless that day, only wanting to talk about her mum's engagement. The previous weekend, Shona told Bryan, Mr Big had taken her mum up in a hot air balloon. She'd stayed in a tent on the ground, and watched her mum float away. While they were up there, Mr Big apparently whipped out a ring and asked Shona's mum to marry him. She'd practically fallen out of the balloon in excitement, Shona said, and by the time they came back down to earth it was all decided.

"He gave my mum this ring with the biggest diamond!" Shona boasted at lunch. Bryan peeled back the top of his sandwich to take out the cucumber. "And look what he gave me!" She extended her right hand. On the fourth finger was a small silver ring with a red enamelled heart on top. "He said that he's marrying me as well as my mum, so I get a ring as well. But hers goes on the left hand and mine goes on the right. He wants me to change my name to his, too. I'm not sure about that though, I like being Shona Smith. Shona Harris doesn't sound the same."

"You could always hyphenate it, love," Bryan's mum had said. "That's when people stick two last names together. Like Poppy Stuart-Hill in your class."

'Looks like she took up that idea,' Bryan thought in the bus.

His stop was coming up. He jumped off the bus and ran splashily towards the glowing windows of the coffee shop. Stepping inside, his glasses fogged immediately. Wiping his fingers over the lenses, he turned his blurred gaze to the perfect table.

It was occupied.

Bryan hurriedly pulled off his glasses and wiped them properly.

The table was definitely taken and, worse, it looked like it would be for the long run. When he'd come here last week to check the place out, the shop had been virtually empty. He'd had his pick of tables, and it hadn't occurred to him that it would be any different this week. "No scientist reaches a conclusion based on only one sample of evidence," he muttered to himself in his chemistry teacher's precise, high-pitched voice. A person at the nearest table turned around. Flushing, Bryan spun to leave.

Then he spotted a free stool by the window and flung himself towards it. Perching sideways, with his legs angled awkwardly under the table, Bryan realised that the dark day had turned the café's large windows into a mirror reflecting the interior. He could keep a close watch on The Table without looking too much like a stalker. He glanced round nervously. Everyone else here was eating or drinking. They might kick him out if he didn't buy something. He peeled off his sodden jacket and draped it over the stool then approached the counter, clutching his carrier bag and scowling over at his table as he went.

Bryan returned to the stool clutching a packet of chocolate-covered espresso beans and positioned them prominently on the table in front of him. He checked inside his carrier bag again, then leaned it against the window by his feet. He placed his hands either side of the packet of beans and drummed his fingers. Shifting uncomfortably on the stool, he felt the bulge of his phone in his pocket and he pulled it out. He clicked on Twitter and tapped 'Kickoff meeting for #youngenterprise leads today. Get your ideas ready, first team meeting coming soon #conningtonhouse #johncarpenter' and sent it off. His leg juddering, he glanced up at the window again. The Table was still occupied.

Bryan scrolled through the photos in his phone to the one he'd taken that morning. He and Shona could have a good laugh about this. He wondered if her copy was on the wall in her room as well. He peered at his own face. Would Shona recognise him? His hair was still the same bright red, but even he struggled to see the 18-year old he'd become in this 10-year old chubby, freckled face.

Things had changed so fast after Shona's announcement. Suddenly she didn't have to attend after-school club, or breakfast club, any more as her mum had quit her job. Then after half-term she simply didn't come back to school. Bryan's mum told him that Shona had been moved to the private school up on the hill, that her new dad wanted her to get a better education and the other school was nearer her new house. "You can still be friends, though, love," his mum had said comfortingly. "There are still weekends."

They'd tried. Bryan would phone Shona but she was so full of her new life, new friends and new possessions that he felt he had little to say. After a while he realised that he was the one always initiating the phone calls so he'd stopped for a while to see if she'd call him. She hadn't. Those last months of primary school on his own had been a welter of misery as Bryan hovered on the edges of the established friendship groups, neither rejected nor welcomed and never quite belonging.

The last time he'd seen Shona had been during the summer before starting secondary school in Bryan's last attempt to keep in touch. They'd met at the park and Shona had showed him her new mobile phone, her new iPod and her new handbag. But when Bryan had led Shona over to their den under the oak tree she'd refused to sit down, saying it would make her pink jeans dirty. She and her mum had left soon after and he hadn't seen her again.

Bryan returned his attention to the window, his leg juddering spasmodically. If he squinted, he could make out shapes outside at the same time as watching the inside of the café. The rainy roads were busy with cars and people huddled under umbrellas. As he watched, a white Mini sped past close to the kerb, throwing up a wall of spray onto some unlucky pedestrians. Bryan smiled in sympathy and folded up one leg to feel the bottom of his still-soaking jeans. He shifted his focus back to The Table. They were moving!

Bryan scooped up the carrier bag, his phone and the espresso beans. He focused firmly on his destination and didn't notice his wet carrier bag brushing against the back of someone's head as he lurched anxiously toward his favoured corner. Before the couple had fully stood up from the table he thrust his carrier bag on top of it and slid into the farthest seat.

"Would you jump in my grave as quick?" the man asked.

"Shush, come on," said the lady with a nervous glance at Bryan's hooded face.

Bryan checked the time on his phone. She should be here soon. He tapped out a text: 'Hi Shona, am in coffee shop, can I order you smthing to drink? //Bryan'

***

Shona drove the Mini down the high street and swerved into the supermarket car park. "Hang on a sec, Emily, just parking," she shouted into the hands-free microphone. "This car park is a bloody nightmare."

She backed the car into a parent-and-child space and switched off the ignition. "OK, Em, I can concentrate now. So what did you find out?"

Emily's voice came tinnily over the speaker. "My mum phoned the director. Apparently we got marked down last year in *Young Enterprise* for being too exclusive. They thought our entry didn't have mass appeal. So that's why they've paired us with John Carpenter School this time, to broaden our reach, they said."

"To dumb us down, more like," Shona sighed. "Why'd we have to go mass market the year I'm leading the team? It's not fair."

"So have you met up with their dear leader yet?"

"No, I'm supposed to be there now, just gearing myself up. Remember our deal; if you haven't heard from me in an hour, you need to come dig me out."

"Don't be so dramatic, how bad can he be? Anyway, didn't you say you know him?"

"According to my mum, we were at primary school together before she married my Dad. I don't remember much about it, though, it was ages ago."

Emily laughed. "You can catch up on the good old days with glue sticks and glitter, they're probably still using those at John Carpenter anyway. Off you go, then, and call me as soon as you're done."

"One hour, Em. Sixty minutes. I'm counting on you."

Shona hung up the phone and immediately it buzzed with a text. She checked the screen. He was there already. She quickly tapped an answer and climbed reluctantly from the car, belting her white raincoat more tightly around her.

***

Bryan stared at his phone: 'Soz running late hot water plz cu in 10 Shona x'

'Hot water?' he thought. 'Can you even order hot water? Do they charge for it? Are they going to let me take up a table if she just has hot water?'

At least he'd bought the beans. He pulled out the packet and placed it in the centre of the table. Maybe he should open them, ready to share. He tore a corner open with his teeth and laid the packet in the centre of the table, poking his fingers in to widen the hole. Suddenly the packet split widely and the beans burst out in a glossy brown bundle, rolling across the table. "Shit!" Bryan muttered, then flushed and shifted his chair slightly as the lady at the next table turned around.

He frantically grabbed after the beans and pushed them back onto the cellophane wrapper. Sticky from the damp table and his fingerprints, now they looked more like a pile of rabbit droppings than a sophisticated snack. Bryan lifted his hand and licked off a couple of beans that had stuck to his fingers, and crunched them noisily. They still tasted all right. He pinched up another few beans and popped them in his mouth, pushed back his hood and returned to the counter.

"Ummm, hot water, please?" he asked tentatively.

"Lemon?" the barista asked.

"Ummm, I don't know. It's not for me. She's not here yet. I don't really know her, I'm not sure . . . do people usually have lemon?" Bryan stuttered, feeling his face redden again.

"I put lemon on the side, yes?" the barista said kindly. "Then your girlfriend, she can choose."

"She's not my girlfriend!" Bryan said. He shoved himself away from the counter and stood rigidly as the barista turned to make the drink. A cold gust of air hit sharply on the nape of his neck as the door opened, and he turned to look.

It must be her. Bryan stared dumbly as the tall girl pushed back the shiny white hood of her raincoat to expose a tumble of blonde curls piled on her head. She shook some raindrops from her sleeves and glanced confidently around the shop. She looked as if a drop of ice cream had never passed her lips.

'No-one here I know,' Shona thought thankfully. She tucked her red leather folder under her arm and looked toward the counter. She started at the intense stare from the boy standing there, ignoring the barista proffering a tall white mug. Shona stepped forward.

"Bryan, right? My mum reminded me of what you looked like. Is that my hot water?"

Bryan jumped and turned to the barista, mutely taking the mug and passing it to Shona. Her fingers brushed against his as she took it.

"Where are we sitting?" she asked.

"I've got a table," Bryan muttered and smiled, exposing small brown shards of espresso bean caught in his teeth. Shona turned away to look in the direction of his pointing finger. Bryan took a small step closer to her and daringly placed his hand on her back to guide her forward. She felt his hand through the back of her raincoat. She hoped he wouldn't leave a stain.

MOCHA

by Liz Losty

JAMIE checked the time on his mobile and realised he needed to rush if he wasn't to keep his mother waiting. He grabbed his jacket, told his boss he was taking the late lunch they had agreed and walked to the coffee shop to meet his mother. It was quiet as the lunch crowd had left and the late afternoon rush was yet to start. He was early and his mother hadn't arrived yet, so Jamie ordered a mocha for himself and the usual skinny cappuccino for his mother. Then he sat down and worked through all the possible reasons his mother would have for wanting to meet him now, not waiting until he got home that evening. He stirred his mocha while he assessed her possible motives. He was clinical in his appraisal. He had learnt to keep his emotional distance from both his parents after all the anger and turmoil of recent months.

Jamie knew as soon as his mother called him that something was wrong. Not because she sounded worried, but because she sounded so bright and breezy.

She hadn't been bright and breezy in months. Not since his dad decided to have his mid-life crisis in such a spectacularly selfish way. Jamie was still living at home and was the reluctant witness to the arguments, the door slamming, his father leaving and his mother breaking. He felt out of his depth, trying to comfort his mother, making her cups of tea, offering to do jobs in the house, the food shopping, helping in any way he could except the one way he knew she needed. He refused to discuss his father's actions, his decision to leave or his selfishness and, most of all, he refused to discuss Emma.

All of those topics were off bounds as far as Jamie was concerned and, while it took some forceful behaviour on his part, his mother finally got the message and stopped asking him how much he had known and how he felt about it all.

The truth was Jamie knew a lot more than he pretended, and he felt pretty wretched about having that knowledge. He had never told his mother any of it and, in truth, he actually resented her for being so stupid and gullible, for loving his father so much that she didn't question any of his actions until the affair became public.

Jamie had found out about it by accident weeks before his mother knew what was going on. He had called into his father's office one Thursday evening at about seven, hoping to get a lift home with him. Someone who was leaving recognised Jamie and held the door open so he didn't need to ask his father to let him in. Most of the building was empty by that time of day, but his father had been working late every night for the last month on a complex project so Jamie knew he would still be there.

Jamie walked towards his father's office, where the lights were still on, and saw him through the blinds, bending over his desk. It was only as he got closer he realised Emma was lying on the desk. Jamie froze, horrified, shocked but most of all disgusted. He didn't want to be witness to what he was seeing.

"Dad!" he shouted in anger. His father jumped back and Emma slid off the desk, smoothing her clothes and pulling her hair back into a pony tail. His father walked swiftly towards the door.

"Jamie, is that you? Hello! What brings you here?" he asked, full of bluff and smiles, smoothing his shirt and running a hand through his thinning hair. His father was obviously a more practised liar than Jamie. He could do nothing to disguise his emotions and just stood silently looking from his father to Emma, the pain and realisation of what he had just witnessed etched clearly on his face.

The awkwardness of that moment lasted to this day. Jamie had eventually come to terms with the knowledge that his father was not the pillar of the community, the solid trustworthy and honourable man Jamie had always believed him to be. Prior to the divorce, his father had tried a couple of times to formally introduce him to Emma so that they 'could get to know each other properly'. Jamie stared at his father in frank disgust when he suggested this.

In a final attempt to win Jamie round, his father had arranged to meet him for lunch. It was only when Jamie got there that he realised with horror that Emma was joining them. She was dressed in a tight-fitting pencil skirt and a silk blouse that was a little too transparent. Jamie couldn't help looking and then blushed when she caught his eye; he had quickly looked away. His father smiled, misinterpreting Jamie's embarrassment for wolfish interest in Emma. She excused herself to go to the ladies room.

"Well! Looks like Emma has another admirer," Andrew smiled, his face slightly flushed from the bottle of wine he had already finished off before the main course arrived.

Jamie turned from watching Emma walk away and looked his father straight in the eye, without speaking, until he stopped smiling.

"What? What's wrong with you now?" Andrew asked impatiently.

"What's wrong with me? With me?" Jamie was almost shouting. "If you ever try and seat me at the same table as that, that . . . " Jamie hesitated over the words, " . . . that home-wrecking bitch ever again, I will tell her exactly what I think of her. She looks like she would make more money dancing around a pole in a club, rather than answering the phones in your office. Still she seems to have done all right out of you hasn't she? Maybe she isn't as stupid as she looks." Jamie spat out the words, not caring who in the restaurant heard, and hoping that Emma was one of them.

"Now look here Jamie . . . " Andrew started. But he didn't get to finish as Jamie had already stormed away from the table, knocking his chair over as he left. He didn't stop as he strode past Emma who was returning, her fixed smile faltering as she saw the look on Jamie's face.

"Stay away," he hissed as he strode past her, clipping her shoulder deliberately with his so that he knocked her off-balance in her too-high heels.

"Jamie!" he could hear his father call after him in admonishment. He didn't look round and was oblivious to the stares of other diners as he stormed out.

He had never told his mother about the events of that day, of his father's tactless plan to win him round, trying to trick him into playing happy families with Emma, trying to force him to accept this new family, so different from the one he had grown up with. While Jamie did not want to be drawn into the arguments between his mother and father, or to take sides, deep down he despised his father for his betrayal, his selfishness and most of all his abandonment of the family life they had.

So he made the decision to stay on in the family home, living with his mother, while making plans for his future life. He did continue to see his father but never Emma. He had eventually agreed to meet his father every Friday for what was usually an uncomfortable and awkward one hour lunch. Jamie always arrived on the dot of one and left sharply at two. Even his punctuality was directed as a silent insult to his father – 'you can have one hour of my time and not a minute longer'. Their conversation was always stilted and confined to safe topics, but even the weather and holidays somehow came loaded with references to a former, distant, happy family life or to Emma.

Jamie had a sense of foreboding when his mother had called him. He knew something was wrong and dreaded what it may be. The past few months had cemented his determination to switch his university place from a local college to one in Europe – far away from both of them and the chance to escape all of the constant feelings of dread that his parents seemed now to represent. He had so looked forward to having this year out and the chance to earn some money. He wished now he had gone straight to university.

He looked up as the door to the coffee shop opened. His mother arrived on time, unusually for her, and sat down while looking around her. "Oh good, at least it's quiet," she said. She dropped some expensive-looking bags at her feet. She had obviously been shopping in some of the high-end boutiques in the old town before meeting him. Despite her chic appearance, his mother had become very frugal after the divorce settlement. To see her spend on anything was unusual. Jamie noted the designer names and wondered why she had suddenly decided to splash out. Then even more unusually she came straight to the point.

"Jamie. You and I have never had secrets and, while there may be some things I should keep from you, I am afraid this is one secret that you will find out about one way or another." Jamie's heart sank as he realised it was to be yet another bombshell of bad news.

And so it was that she told Jamie about his father and Emma and the baby that they were expecting. And Jamie kept sipping his mocha to make sure he could still breathe and swallow and to stop himself screaming out the anger and hatred he felt for his father.

"God I really do wish he was dead," Jamie muttered through tight lips.

"Jamie! Don't say that. I know it's a shock and really upsetting, believe me I do know that, but please don't wish him dead. He is still your father." Kate surprised herself with the words. She realised now how Helen must have felt when she had uttered the same words. It was suddenly shocking to hear someone wish death on the person they once loved.

"I can't believe you, Mum. Even you wanted him dead – so don't preach to me about how I should feel and react." Jamie had begun to raise his voice and some people nearby had turned to see who was shouting.

"Jamie, don't. Please don't. I don't deserve your anger. Of course you're upset, and your father should certainly have told you himself, but please don't be angry with me. I just wanted you to know because you have a right to know, it is as simple as that." Kate reached a hand out to touch Jamie's arm. He flinched and made to pull away, but she grabbed his arm more firmly and looked into his eyes.

"It will be alright Jamie. He does still love you. No matter what has happened between your father and I, and that . . . girl." Kate knew how much damage had already been done to Jamie. His sudden angry outbursts, the occasional heavy drinking, the sullen presence in her house. He had changed so much, she didn't want him to change any more.

"Jamie, please look at me. We do both still love you. You are loved. Your father having another baby, well it's difficult for you, of course it is. But don't doubt his love for you, it doesn't mean he will love you any less." Kate knew she was repeating herself, but she wanted to ensure Jamie heard the most important word again and again.

Jamie looked up at her, then glanced around. He watched the other people in the coffee shop, laughing, chatting, waiting, reading or drinking, all in seemingly happy oblivion to the pain he felt. He would realise looking back on that day, that this was adulthood, this was when he truly became a man and his own person. He was no longer a child, could no longer go back or count on the security and unconditional love of his parents. Most of all he realised he couldn't count on his father, who may love him but not enough to keep the family together. That was all Jamie had wanted. No, his father had chosen to go off and create a new family, a new wife, a new child. Jamie's sense of rejection could never be overcome by his father's supposed love.

Kate watched Jamie's face as he struggled to compute this information and what it would mean for him.

"Does that mean I will have a brother or a sister – or a half-brother? Is she now my step-mother? Is he actually that serious, are they getting married?" The questions were fired quickly at Kate as Jamie's mind worked through all the implications.

"You can call him or her what you want, and who knows if they will get married," Kate replied. "But the thing about having children is that it changes everything." Jamie realised that he had been changed by his father's carelessness, or was it Emma's cunning? He didn't think the baby was his father's idea. He was too selfish to want a baby in his life at his age.

"We'll be okay Jamie, you and I," Kate reassured him. "We've come through lots over the years and we can both get through this. You'll soon be off to university, having a whale of a time and you will be away from all this unpleasantness. You will have your own life."

Jamie looked at her, his face registering his resignation to the latest debacle his father had managed to introduce. "Well, good luck to him, Mum, that's all I can say. He was a crap Dad to me and he will be to this kid too. He never came to any of my school sports days and he never collected me from school. He was always busy with work. If he does show up when this kid is at school they'll think he's the granddad! No fool like an old fool." Jamie sipped his mocha and looked at his mother with a wry smile.

DECAF
SINGLE ESPRESSO
by Vicky Trelinska

SOPHIE looked round the coffee shop. She liked to check, before she bought a drink, that seats were available. She didn't want to stand, but the café was almost empty. Only one other customer was there, an old man working on his laptop.

"What can I get you?" asked the man behind the counter. The manager, she assumed, as he was wearing a suit. There weren't any other staff around.

She ached for a ristretto but instead she said, "A decaf single espresso and a glass of water, please."

She patted herself on the back. It was five days since she'd gone cold turkey and stopped drinking caffeine. The headaches, that no over-the-counter pain killer would relieve, had finally stopped but she felt half asleep and the longing for caffeine continued.

Her GP thought coffee was causing the palpitations and irregular heart beat that often made her feel faint and frightened her. Recently giving a song recital she'd nearly fainted when the palpitations started quite unexpectedly. She'd leant against the grand piano and gripped the lid until the feeling passed. Luckily, it happened at the end of *Phydilé* by Duparc so it looked as if she was recovering after the outpouring of emotion.

"Anything else?" The Danish pastries were inviting but she wasn't hungry; it would just be comfort eating.

"No thanks." She gave herself a brownie point for resisting temptation. It would be silly to eat and find her singing affected. The audition this evening was important. Although she wouldn't finish her course at the Conservatoire until the end of June she needed to start filling her diary with work for the summer. If she didn't get singing engagements she would have to find a job of some kind otherwise she would have no money. If she was offered something in the Bach Festival she was auditioning for, it would give her two weeks work at the beginning of July. The conductor, Charles Frost, was well-known. She didn't mind whether it was in the chorus or as a soloist – either would look good on her CV and, if she impressed him, it was likely she would be offered more work which would help pay that month's rent.

"Take a seat," said the manager. "I'll bring it over."

She had an hour to wait. Her friend, Colin, told her she mustn't be early. He'd arrived at Charles Frost's house ten minutes early yesterday for his audition. When he rang the bell, the front door was opened and a clock thrust in his face. The door slammed shut and he was left holding the clock for ten minutes. He felt that standing on a doorstep in October for ten minutes breathing in cold air had affected his voice and he hadn't sung well. He didn't think he'd be offered anything.

Sophie went over to a table and took out her music. She'd use the time to go over the arias she'd chosen to sing and do some gentle humming to warm up her voice. She had the usual St Matthew Passion and B Minor Mass with her but she'd also brought Bach's Coffee Cantata. It would be something different. She'd performed the soprano arias recently at the Conservatoire with a group of students. Colin had taken the tenor role. She rather fancied Colin. She thought he liked her but he hadn't asked her out yet. Maybe she could help things along and suggest they did some duets together. She smiled as she imagined going out for a drink after they'd rehearsed, and wondered where they'd go.

Her daydream was interrupted by the manager bringing her coffee. Sophie took a sip. Thank goodness it was hot. If there was one thing she couldn't stand it was lukewarm coffee. She was pleased he had remembered her glass of water. She loved the Viennese habit of drinking water with coffee. It was in Vienna two years ago where she'd attended a summer school that her addiction to coffee had begun. There'd been plenty of spare time and she and her friends had spent hours sampling all the Viennese cafés and the different coffees. She'd found the ones with whipped cream too rich. The strong, black ones were her favourite.

She looked at the first soprano aria in the Coffee Cantata but there were too many references to the drink and its lovely flavour so she shut the score. It reminded her of the surge a hit of strong coffee gave. The feeling of being wide awake, alive, ready for anything as, like rocket fuel, it blasted you into higher realms. She turned to the B Minor Mass but, instead of the opening of the Laudamus te, all she could think of was the Cantata and strong coffee.

"Come on. Concentrate," she muttered to herself, and tried again.

"May I join you?" Sophie looked up. It was Theresa, the last person she wanted to be with right now. Tall and slim with long, thick dark hair, Theresa was the sort who could hike across Dartmoor on a wet, windy cold day and still look as if she was heading for a night at the Oscars. She was wearing a Ralph Lauren navy blue coat and an Armani scarf. Somehow Theresa always managed to let everyone know where she'd bought her clothes and just how expensive they were. 'It's easy to look like a model,' Sophie thought with a twinge of jealously, 'when you're tall and slim and your father gives you a large allowance.' Sophie had no such family backing and was short and chubby. She always felt dowdy when she was with Theresa.

Theresa had come to the Conservatoire the previous year after doing a BMus degree at Oxford. She thought she knew more and was better informed about music than those who'd only studied at the Conservatoire and was always showing off her knowledge. Sophie knew she wasn't, having caught her out once or twice on such things as the current way of performing trills.

The problems between them had really started after Sophie had let slip in front of Theresa that David, a string player, had asked her out. When David cancelled the date with Sophie saying he had to work she hadn't minded; she would have done the same. But when Sophie found out he hadn't been working and had taken Theresa out instead she was very upset. She hadn't said anything to David. She just assumed he preferred Theresa and was just too embarrassed to say.

Then there was the time Sophie had told Theresa the fee she was getting for a job. A few days later the conductor told Sophie he wouldn't be using her. Later she'd seen a poster for the concert with Theresa's name in the part Sophie had been asked to perform. Putting a few feelers out she discovered Theresa was being paid less than Sophie had asked for. Sophie put it down to experience and resolved never to tell anyone again what she was being paid.

Rumours were going around about Theresa as others found they'd lost out to her. Sophie didn't like anyone being underhand and devious. She considered there was plenty of work for everyone; each person had their own worth. If you were good you would get engagements. If you weren't then, to start with, you might get on by being ruthless and trampling over others but in the long run it wouldn't do you any good.

Realising that Theresa was still waiting for an answer, Sophie gritted her teeth and, hoping her smile didn't look too false, said "Yes, do join me. Are you auditioning for the Bach Festival as well?"

"Charles rang last week and invited me to come. He hinted it was really a formality and he was pretty sure he'd have something for me."

'Charles is it?' thought Sophie, to whom he was Mr Frost. Theresa was always name-dropping, but Sophie wasn't sure that Theresa really did know the people as well as she made out.

The manager brought Theresa's herb tea over. "Would you like another?" he asked Sophie.

"Yes, please." She was grateful he hadn't specified what coffee she was drinking. If Theresa knew she was on decaf it would be all round the Conservatoire by tomorrow that Sophie, who was renowned for not being able to function without regular doses of caffeine throughout the day, was now drinking decaf. Sophie imagined the spin Theresa would put on it. She'd make out Sophie's palpitations were caused by nerves and that Sophie was unable to get on a platform without fainting. Sophie imagined how Theresa would sound very concerned, offering her help and advice, whilst scheming to take over all her engagements.

Theresa pointed to the score of the Coffee Cantata. "You're like a junkie with heroin when it comes to coffee. It won't be one of the works Charles will be performing. He doesn't like it."

"I'm taking all the usual works; the B Minor, Matthew Passion. I just thought I'd offer it as something different and let him choose what he wanted to hear."

"He likes people to be decisive and know what they want to sing. He told me last week how much he appreciated that I knew what I sang well and how I instinctively sensed what suited my voice."

Theresa was interrupted by the manager bringing Sophie's drink. She hunched over the cup, warming her hands round it. Was she imagining it and being over-sensitive or was Theresa deliberately setting out to undermine her?

"Have you heard from Summer Opera yet?" asked Theresa. They had both auditioned for it last week. If accepted it meant four weeks paid work in August.

"No. Not yet."

"That's odd I heard on Friday that I'd got into the chorus. I shouldn't worry about it. There's still plenty of time to find work before we leave the Conservatoire. You might get something in the Bach Festival, although I would have thought your voice was too operatic for Bach. Charles says he likes clear, pure voices like mine with very little vibrato."

Sophie fiddled with the coffee spoon and put it back in the saucer. She couldn't trust herself not to poke it in Theresa's eye.

"In my opinion you'd be much better concentrating on opera rather than Bach," said Theresa.

'Who cares about your opinion?' thought Sophie. Her shoulders drooped. She felt her confidence draining away. "We'll have to be going soon," she said. "I'll just go to the loo."

Once on her own Sophie looked at herself in the mirror. 'For goodness sake,' she thought. 'Pull yourself together. Don't let this woman get at you. She's only trying to build up her own confidence at your expense. Come on, be positive. You can do it. You know you're good. Stand up straight. Look as if you are in control.' Sophie stood up, pulled her shoulders back. 'Now go out there, ignore her and get on with the job.'

When Sophie got back to the table her phone rang. She looked at it. The call was from the administrator at Summer Opera.

"Don't answer it. We haven't time. Charles hates unpunctuality," said Theresa.

"I have to take this. It's important. Hallo . . . Yes, I'm Sophie Small . . . I see . . . Yes, of course . . . Thank you."

Sophie smiled as she ended the call. Looking directly at Theresa and trying not to sound smug and self-satisfied she said, "That was Summer

Opera. They've offered me small parts in all the productions."

Theresa drew in a sharp breath.

"Come on, let's go," said Sophie, as Theresa sat staring with her mouth open.

Sophie strode to the door aware that Theresa hadn't congratulated her. Now she really felt in control and confident. No amount of caffeine could have given her this feeling of well-being and confidence in her abilities. She was wide awake and raring to go. Let Theresa do her worst, this was going to be her night.

FLAT WHITE

by Linda Cohen

LIBBY sat in the coffee shop, watching the door intently. She wondered whether he would actually come. Surely he would, but who knows? Maybe he'll get cold feet at the last moment, maybe it was just some trick and he had no intention of coming. 'Come on, Libby,' she reassured herself. 'Why else would he have written to you?'

The letter had come completely out of the blue, changing everything for her in just a moment. As she turned it over in her hand and read it for the umpteenth time, she wondered whether someone had written it for him.

Dear Libby,

I hope you don't mind me contacting you like this, but I believe you are my sister. I have been trying to trace you for many years now, but finally think I may have a breakthrough. I wondered whether you would like to meet up, and maybe we could try and fill in some of the gaps of the years behind us. I note the town you live in, and I am not that far away from you. If you are happy to, shall we meet at a coffee shop?

Hoping this letter finds you well, and that you will agree to a meeting.

Yours Jake (formerly known as Jack)

When the letter had first arrived she had been overcome with emotion and had not told anyone. Now everyone knew she was finally going to meet the little brother from whom she had been torn apart when she was six and he was three.

Today was the day. After several days of trying to contact him on the mobile number he had given her she had finally managed to get hold of him. They had had an uncomfortable conversation: only to be expected, Libby told herself. Once they met she was sure things would revert to how they had been all those years ago. She smiled fondly when she remembered a little blonde, blue-eyed boy, always with a scab on his knee, a runny nose and grubby clothes, but what could you expect with a feckless mother like theirs? Libby had been lucky. After being put into care she had been adopted by the Morrisons, the sweetest couple she could ever have wished for. Not a day went by that she didn't give thanks for their love over the years. Now they were both dead, her adoptive father first, then her loving wonderful adoptive mother. How she missed them, missed their kindness and advice, missed their wonderful home that she could run back to any time that she wanted. She wondered what had happened to Jack. She had lost touch with him completely and now, out of the blue, this letter. She read it through one more time.

She checked her watch – it was nearly three o'clock, the time they had agreed to meet. She felt nervous about meeting him, nervous about what to say, nervous about how she looked. She hoped what she was wearing was right. She felt she should look sophisticated but not over the top; a silk blouse, straight pencil skirt, medium heels and the Mulberry bag she had treated herself to all those years ago when she had been made a partner in the law firm. What an achievement: her parents had been so proud. They had all gone out for dinner to celebrate and her parents told her how pleased they were. The love she felt for them flowed over her that night.

Libby settled herself at a convenient table where she had a good view of people coming into the coffee shop. The door opened several times but she knew none of them were him, not that she was sure she would recognise him. She was thirty-three and he would be thirty. How strange to think that, after so many years apart, at last they could be together.

Suddenly the door was flung open and in walked a tall scruffy-looking individual wearing a beanie hat, unwashed hair sticking out from underneath it, and clothes that looked like they hadn't seen the inside of a washing machine for a very long time. The man stood, looked around with an air of indifference, sniffed, then spotted her. There was an uncomfortable exchange of recognition, and Libby found herself feeling disappointed. She didn't really know what she had expected, but certainly someone a bit smarter looking than this. He came over to her table, and stood looking down at her. Libby stood up as if to give him a hug, but he moved away. "Hi," said Libby. "Are you Jake?"

"That's me," he said. "So you are Libby?" He looked approvingly at her, and nodded at her clothes. "You dressed up a bit, didn't you?" he said sarcastically.

"Well, not really," said Libby. "I always dress like this. Please sit down Jake, let me get you a coffee."

"Don't mind if I do," said Jake. "And maybe something to eat at the same time? Ham sandwich or something? Don't suppose they do pies in a place like this, do they?" he added. She noticed that he made no attempt whatsoever to offer to pay for the food, just left it to her.

"So Jake, tell me about yourself and your life," said Libby, returning with the coffees and a sandwich. She tried not to sound too condescending.

"Not much to tell really," said Jake. "Went into care. Several people tried to adopt me, but a few couples just took me back. Couldn't cope with me," he said with a nasty sneer.

"Oh dear. Why was that?" asked Libby.

"Well, I hate do-gooders," said Jake. "And I didn't mind it in care. It was quite fun sometimes. Got to do whatever we liked. Met some great people just like myself, they were always up for a laugh – running away and all that, sleeping in doorways then being hauled back when we were caught. As I said, bit of a laugh really." Libby thought it sounded anything but a laugh, and wondered how she could find some common ground between them.

"I was so excited when I got your letter," she said. "I couldn't sleep for days. How long have you been trying to find me?"

"Oh, a while," said Jake. "Then one thing led to another, and here we are. You look like you've done ok for yourself. Proper posh, not at all what I expected."

"I've been lucky," Libby replied. "I had the most wonderful adoptive parents, who encouraged me all the way, managed to get a degree and here I am." Libby felt slightly uncomfortable by what she perceived as showing off in Jake's eyes, until she noticed that he wasn't really listening.

"So did you ever see the old girl again after we went into care?" asked Jake.

"No," said Libby, sadly. "She never wanted contact. Did you?"

"Nah!" Jake snorted. "Nor would I ever have wanted to." Libby couldn't really blame him. Bad memories came flooding back to her as they were talking, of Jake being pulled by his hair, their mother reeking of whisky, and yet another 'Uncle' coming out of her bedroom at some ungodly hour.

"It was awful, wasn't it Jake? It's amazing that we have come out of it all unscathed."

"Speak for yourself," said Jake. "I don't feel unscathed. That woman wrecked my life. What a nightmare, and she had the cheek to call herself a mother." Libby couldn't help thinking that they had both had the same beginning but she had managed to pull herself up by her boot straps and had made something of her life, with the help of her amazing parents. Jake, on the other hand, looked completely down and out and she felt very sad.

Just as she was about to ask Jake for a bit more information about himself there was a loud argument at the table next to theirs. A woman was shouting and getting angry. Libby wondered what it was all about. Jake began to laugh. "Blimey, wouldn't like to be sitting at that table. Sounds like something that used to go on at our house Libby, except a lot posher."

Libby smiled, remembering how it used to be: the shouting and hitting, the mental abuse. The only reason she could smile at the memory was because everything had changed for her when her wonderful new parents took over.

"Would you like to see a photograph of my parents?" asked Libby. "I carry them with me always in this locket. They gave it to me shortly before they died. It's all I have left of them, so it is really very special to me."

Jake nodded. She opened a beautiful locket to show him the parents of whom she was so proud. Libby noticed that Jake hardly glanced at the photograph, but turned the locket over and over in his hands. She suddenly felt uneasy, and took it from him, putting it back in her bag.

'Maybe he just isn't interested in them,' she thought. After all, he didn't seem to have any lovely memories of his own.

Libby noticed that Jake had already devoured his sandwich and coffee and was looking around for more. "Would you like something else?" she asked him.

"Thought you'd never ask." His insolence unnerved her. She realised he probably had no money on him and may not have eaten well for days. His air of nonchalance cloaked his insecurity – and hunger. Libby felt tears of disappointment pricking at the back of her eyes.

"I'm just going to get myself another flat white. Is there anything else you would like?" asked Libby, knowing the answer.

"Oh well, another sandwich wouldn't go amiss," said Jake. "Don't suppose they do pies or chips here, do they?"

"No, I don't think so," said Libby.

"I'll have a hot chocolate at the same time," said Jake. Libby felt herself fuming inside. It was a long way from the delightful little boy she had loved as a baby to this big scruffy individual who claimed to be her brother. She wondered how she was ever going to get out of this situation. So many times in the past she had imagined their meeting again: how they would fall into each other's arms, talk sadly of their past yet regale each other with tales of how they had managed to rise above it all, and just see how successful they had both become. This, she realised, was simply the stuff of dreams and not reality at all. The reality was that her dear little brother had grown up into a masculine version of their mother, and that was certainly no good.

"I'll just go and get us something else to eat and drink," said Libby, trying to sound cheerful.

"Righto," said Jake, looking into the distance. "I'll just sit here and wait." Libby felt anger welling up inside her. How dare he just assume she would keep feeding him like this. Didn't he have any pride? Didn't he care at all about her or feel proud of all that she had achieved, despite their dreadful start in life? All these thoughts crowded into Libby's head whilst she waited at the counter for their food and drinks. The coffee shop was really busy now, but at least it gave her time to think. Maybe she was being unfair: after all he had not been lucky like her. She must be more tolerant, try and find out more about him and how he had managed.

At last she was at the counter. She ordered their drinks and asked if they served chips. She wasn't surprised that they didn't, so she asked for a bag of salt and vinegar crisps together with more ham and cheese sandwiches. She turned to go back to her table, and could not see him. 'That's strange,' she thought. 'Where is he?' She tried to choke down a feeling of apprehension.

Their table was empty and her bag was gone. Libby felt tears start to pour down her face, not for the first time today. 'This can't be happening – I don't believe it,' she thought. She put the tray down on the table and ran to the door. Jake was nowhere to be seen. She rushed back and asked if anybody had seen what happened. Nobody had. Several people tutted in sympathy but no-one was really bothered. She sat at the table and castigated herself for taking her purse out of her bag to pay for the food rather than taking the whole bag with her. Her parents had always warned her that she was too trusting, but Jake was her brother. Surely she should have been able to trust him?

Now she was in a dilemma. Should she call for the police, or should she just accept what had happened? But how could she come to terms with the loss of her precious locket and the photographs? She didn't care about the bag – she could buy a new one – but how could she ever replace the locket? Despair ran through her – she just could not believe what had happened to her. She sat with her head in her hands, trying to calm her thoughts and decide what to do.

Suddenly she heard the chair opposite her scrape back. "Sorry about that." She looked up, and there was Jake. "Had to see a man about a dog," he smiled. "I didn't want to leave your bag hanging there so I took it with me, especially as you told me how precious your locket was. Can't take any chances these days can you?" Libby couldn't believe it. She felt guilty that she could have thought these awful things about Jake, and relieved that her locket was safe.

"Oh Jake," she cried. "I thought you'd left."

"Why would I do that?" he asked in surprise. "We've only just found each other."

She didn't dare tell him how she suspected he had stolen her bag, how he was a thoroughly bad lot, and how she was worried he was just like their mother. He stared at her for a moment, and then realised what she had been thinking.

"Libby I know what I look like but I can assure you I am nothing like her. I may look rough, and things have been hard, but I do have principles – and I wouldn't ever steal from anyone, let alone my sister. I hope you know that."

Libby looked shamefaced as she stared at the brother who was a stranger to her. "Jake, can you ever forgive me? I didn't know what to think, and I should have known better."

Jake sighed. "Don't blame you thinking that way. After all, look at you and look at me. If the boot were on the other foot I would have thought the same." His eyes suddenly lit up. "Crisps," he said. "Not quite chips, but you got crisps!"

"Yes," said Libby.

"Let's just forget about the other business, and start all over again," suggested Jake. Libby smiled, and for a while was looking straight into the face of her three-year-old brother.

A CUP OF TEA

by Emma Dark

ANNA walked past the coffee shop at least three times. She glanced through the window to make sure there weren't too many people inside and that there were none of those young professionals who know what they want and order with white-toothed confidence. Some people, she noticed, were sitting alone. Even after all this time she had to be absolutely certain that he was not there.

She was still finding it hard to go out alone. She would look at the shops and, if she felt confident enough, would stop for a quiet cup of tea somewhere. She opened the door and, keeping her eyes on the floor to avoid eye contact, went to the counter. A young waitress behind the counter smiled at her as she approached and asked her what she would like. Anna noticed the girl's accent but could not place it.

"Just a cup of tea please."

"What tea?" the waitress asked.

"Just normal tea."

"Normal tea?" repeated the waitress, looking puzzled.

"Yes, just brown ordinary tea."

"Yes, but what type of tea?"

The waitress was pointing to a board behind the counter. As Anna looked up to scrutinise it she became aware of a queue forming behind her. The familiar sensations of anxiety began to take hold as she read the long list of teas she could have. English Breakfast, Assam, Earl Grey, Fruit tea, Green tea, Camomile, Peppermint: the list went on.

Anna had to make a decision, but making decisions for herself was not her strong point; someone else was always there to make these decisions for her. She was ashamed: thirty-five years old and incapable of even ordering a cup of tea. She was everything he had said, stupid and useless, and now she was making a fool of herself in front of people she didn't know and they would laugh at her. She tried to hear what her therapist would say: 'I am over-generalising, I am labelling', but it didn't seem to help in this pressurised situation. Saying the first thing that came into her mind, she said, "I'll have a coffee." Anna could feel her heart start to pound.

"OK, what type of coffee would you like?" asked the waitress as she pointed to an even longer list of possible coffees. Anna wanted to run, but her legs would not move. She felt out of breath and tears were gathering in her eyes.

"I'm so sorry," she said. "I'll pay anyway."

"You can't pay if you haven't ordered."

Anna rummaged frantically in her handbag for her purse which, of course, she could not find. A smartly dressed woman behind her tapped her foot on the floor. Anna dropped her bag and everything spilled out. She dropped to the floor, hurriedly scooped her belongings back into the bag and stood up. She was going to flee, leaving her bag and everything in the coffee shop, when an older waitress came up to her. She put her hand over Anna's and spoke to the younger waitress, kindly.

"She means a cup of English breakfast tea." Anna looked at her: her name badge said *Beryl*.

Darren had heard Anna drop her bag, and he appeared behind the counter. "Is everything okay?" he asked. "Beryl, please show this lady to a table and I'll bring the tea. Please let me offer you one of our cakes on the house as an apology for upsetting and confusing you."

"That's alright," Anna said, and then she added, "Please don't tell her off. It was my fault."

Beryl replied gently, "It wasn't your fault at all. The customer is always right."

As Beryl led her to a quiet table, Anna thought 'I can do it, this kind lady said I was right. I just have to believe I can and stamp on those self-defeating thoughts. The doctors did say there will be times when it is two steps forward and one step back, but I can do it.'

Going out alone was a very big step for Anna, but not as big as the first step. That had been an almost unconscious decision, made by her body to protect itself. She had entered a women's refuge. She had seen the telephone number in her doctor's surgery while she was waiting to get more of the pills that made it possible for her to function. She remembered thinking that the refuge had the same telephone code as her own and might be very near, it might only be a few streets away. She went into the Ladies, got out her mobile and called the number, telling herself she just wanted to know where it was. Of course she would not go there, she had no reason to go there. Her call was answered after the second ring. Anna did not really remember what the woman said, but she remembered her asking 'Are you in a safe place?' There was such understanding in that question that Anna felt able to ask for the address, and she was right: it was only a few streets away. Anna found that her feet took her there while her mind slept. She got as far as the door and hesitated. Her mind woke up and she thought 'What on earth am I doing here?' She found she could not knock but simply stood there. She was about to leave when the door opened.

A large woman said, "Come in love, you're welcome here."

Anna collapsed. She had little memory of what happened next. There was a vague sensation of large strong arms around her, of being carried like a child and then crying like a child. She remembered the warmth of someone's hand holding hers as her sobs slowly subsided; being too tired to speak; sitting by a fire in silence; not having to think of excuses for her behaviour or having to explain anything; being still and quiet while someone made her tea, stewed and milky with lots of sugar; taking the tea from someone who expected no 'thank you', someone who did no more than sit with her. In that silence Anna somehow communicated the years of pain, pain so deep it needed time to surface. She cried and was held tight; she relaxed and more tea was made. No questions were asked. Later she was led to a very small but neat and clean room. It had pale green walls and there was a single bed, beautifully made up. There was a small wash bag by a sink, containing everything an unexpected guest might need – toothbrush, toothpaste, flannel, comb, moisturiser, even a new pair of knickers. There was an old but clean nightdress on the bed.

Anna's attendant left her to get ready for bed. When she came back she said, "I am Geraldine. I am a retired nurse and we have a volunteer policewoman and woman doctor coming in an hour. If you are physically hurt we can treat you. Would you like any type of treatment for physical injury? The decision is yours."

This brought Anna back to reality. She heard the word police and started to speak very quickly.

"Oh no, it wasn't physical. He's not a violent man. He's not a bad man at all. It's me – it's all my fault. He just gets frustrated and says unkind things. I can't do anything right for him. He thinks I'm so stupid and clumsy and I embarrass him. He says I'm lucky to be married to a man like him. Even my father says so. Ted could have had anyone and he chose me but I just mess it up all the time. I say stupid things in front of his friends and family and, worse, his work colleagues. After we see people he goes through everything I said. He makes me see how stupid it sounded and how they will laugh about me when he sees them at work. But then he cuddles me and says he is used to making the best of things. After last week he said it would be better if we stopped having people round. That way I might be able to relax and not be so clumsy. He said it was best for me and that, despite everything, he loves me. I'm his little airhead and he'll never leave me and will always protect me. He says he knows I'll never be like some of his other girlfriends who had good jobs and were very competent at everything they did. He said he wanted a proper wife, a good home-maker, someone who could cook and clean to his standard. I try to do everything to his standard, but I just mess it up. I always do something wrong. He works for my father's company and last week he asked my parents round for dinner with some other colleagues. Everything was fine but then I left the sugar out of the custard and it tasted horrible. After everyone left I thought he would be cross, but he just said 'Six out of ten. You got the main course right but you wouldn't be you if you got everything right. Hell would have to freeze over in the meantime.' He said he would just go to work and make the best of it again. He said he would have to make a joke of it with his colleagues and how they would all laugh at me. I asked him not to tell them but he said it would be all around the office anyway. So you see it's not him, it really is me. I've been like this all my life. I came here today because I saw your ad at the doctors and my feet just brought me here, but I shouldn't be here. I'm wasting your time. I'm not a battered or abused woman. I'm just tired and a bit silly. I'm lucky really, and now I should go. I've just got muddled up again and done the wrong thing as usual. I'm so sorry to have wasted your time. I'm so sorry."

At this point Geraldine took both of Anna's hands in hers and said, "You can go or stay, the decision is yours. There will be no pressure either way from the people here, but I do not think you did the wrong thing today. I think you did exactly the right thing."

Bewilderment crossed Anna's face. No-one had ever said before that she had done the right thing: not her domineering father, not her brow-beaten mother who had never been forgiven for not producing a son and heir, and not Ted, the man she married partly in the hope of pleasing her father and who was now the heir-apparent to her father's business. No-one had ever said that to her. Tiredness overtook Anna: she climbed into bed and slept.

Later that night she woke with a gasp. She had a surge of adrenalin and her heart was pumping. What had she done? She was in so much trouble. She had not told anyone where she was. They might have called the police and they would be looking for her. She must leave immediately. She would leave some money as payment for the room and go as quickly and quietly as possible. She told herself that she was not an abused woman, she was just a little confused at the moment. She had to get home and apologise. Ted would explain it all to her. She could almost hear him say what a silly little airhead she had been. He would look after her and he was right. She had messed up again. No wonder her father and Ted were always irritated by her. When she thought of Geraldine, she was overcome with embarrassment.

Anna switched on her mobile phone and saw many missed messages from Ted. He must be so worried. She started to listen to the first message. It said, "I know you went out today. Call me immediately." Then, "Call me now and I will come and pick you up. What do you think you are playing at?" Then, "I don't know what you think you are doing. I don't want to call your father but I will if I don't hear from you. No doubt you are lost, only you could get lost in your own town.

Call me now." Then, "I called your father. He said don't call the police, it will be too embarrassing. You are just being stupid and hysterical as always. When you get home . . . "

Anna didn't listen to any more. She got dressed and made the bed, leaving thirty pounds on it. She hoped no-one would notice her leaving. She got to the front door and managed the many locks. She ran the few streets to her house and opened the front door. Ted was standing there, and behind him was her father. She saw their faces moving, talking, but she heard nothing. She felt a blast of cold air rush towards her, pushing her back like an icy spike through her chest. The hall light was so bright she could not see. She lost her hearing. She was soaked in her own sweat. She was light-headed and felt her legs give way beneath her. Someone was shouting. She struggled for breath. She was dying and she did not care.

Anna came to in the ambulance for a short time. She remembered an office, then a bed, then nothing. No thoughts, no dreams, just stillness for a very long time.

Later, much later, and from the depths of her memory, Anna felt someone holding her hand and reading The Velveteen Rabbit to her. It had been her favourite childhood story, and she loved it. She looked at the hand holding hers then recognised the voice. It was her mother, but she looked younger and brighter. She was wearing makeup and smart clothes.

"Mum!" Anna said.

"Oh, you're back. I'll call the nurse."

All this was a year ago. Anna was told that she had had a very serious breakdown. There had been therapy sessions, group work, CBT, mindfulness classes, meditation, yoga. There were still gaps in her memory. She did not remember that when her husband visited her in hospital she screamed until he was sent away; neither did she remember that when her father came she tried to hide under the bed. Their visits had been banned by her mother and the doctors. Her mother's quiet presence soothed her. She did not remember being told that her father had died and when she was told again she cried, not from grief but because she could not mourn him. There were long conversations with her mother, who apologised again and again for not standing up to her father and allowing him to bully them and for letting her marry a man who was just like her father. Later she learned that her father had not found time to make a will and so everything had been left to her mother, not to Ted as her father had threatened. Anna moved back in with her mother, who had sacked Ted. Anna was divorcing him: despite his earlier threats, that was turning out to be quite easy. Her mother had sold the business and, with the sale of other assets and investments, they were now wealthy. They were selling the family home which held so many unhappy memories and were looking for somewhere to move to. It would be far away from this town. A very large donation was on its way to the women's refuge.

Anna was still finding it hard to go out alone. But today she sat in the coffee shop with a smile on her face, her hands around the cup that held her stewed milky sweet tea. She kept repeating, "I did it, I did it." She thought that, even though she and her mother were now well-off and she didn't have to work, she might nevertheless one day have the confidence to get a job in a place like this and then she too could say, "The customer is always right."

FILTER COFFEE

by Chris Payne

GERALD stretched out his hand and switched off the alarm before it began to ring. Forty years of rising at precisely the same time each morning had his body clock as precisely tuned as a Swiss watch. Beth teased that he didn't need an alarm at all; she couldn't remember the last time she had heard it. One April Fool's Day she had hidden his clock as a joke. He still remembered the sickening sensation when he reached out his morning hand and felt only empty space where the clock should have been.

He slid quietly from beneath the covers, wincing slightly at the pain in his back. Perhaps it was time to heed his GP's advice and start taking a little more exercise. "Your years at a desk have done you no favours," the doctor had scolded. "You need to start building up an exercise habit. Try golf. Then you'll start looking forward to retirement, and you'll be able to enjoy even more of it."

Gerald edged quietly along the bed, careful not to tread on the bedspread that hung down to the floor. Shutting the bathroom door noiselessly, he switched on the light. It dazzled him to full consciousness as he prepared for his day. He shaved carefully, never meeting his own eyes in the mirror, and smoothed his thin brown hair in a neat side parting. Finally dressing in the suit that hung ready on the back of the bathroom door, he crept softly downstairs. Just before he left the house, he placed an insulated mug of tea on Beth's bedside table and kissed her sleepy forehead, smiling at her mumbled farewell. Downstairs his polished shoes were waiting and he shrugged on his raincoat. He

148

squared up to the hall mirror and adjusted his tie, then placed his hat firmly on his head. He lifted yesterday's post from the hall table, slipped it into his briefcase and finally stepped outside into the damp dark morning, locking the door behind him and testing the handle.

A brisk ten minute walk brought Gerald within sight of the station. The pavements were already busy with the morning's advance guard. Gerald fell into step and moved steadily down the hill towards his destination. He assumed position in the third-door unit with his fellow travellers, whom he had privately christened Scruffy Sue, Nasty Neil and Snoring Stan. After all the years together on this train, he still had no idea of who they really were. Stan swayed upright next to Gerald, who marvelled that the man had enough consciousness to make it to the station each morning. He knew that Stan would stumble blindly to the first seat and snore the whole way to the City.

The train arrived and Gerald stood sideways deferentially to allow Sue on first, but stepped smartly in front of Neil in their wordless competition to be the first male foot on the train. Sue slumped in her accustomed corner and pulled out a bulging makeup bag. Gerald took his own favoured seat and tucked his briefcase on the overhead rack. He leant his forehead against the cool window and let his mind stay blessedly blank.

After nine stops he rose, slid down his briefcase and stepped cautiously to the train's doors, grasping the top of seats and avoiding Stan's sleeping knee protruding into the aisle. Sue was only halfway through her morning makeup ritual. Gerald felt briefly sorry that he never got to see the finished result anymore. He stood alone in the vestibule of the carriage and waited for the train to stop, watching his reflection waver uncertainly in the door's glass as the train slowed.

Soon he was pushing open the heavy door to the coffee shop. As usual, he was the first to arrive and Beryl waved cheerily from behind the counter where she was stacking mugs. "The pot's not quite brewed yet, love," she called. "I'll bring your coffee over in a minute. Take a seat."

Gerald walked to the far corner and removed his raincoat, folding it carefully and laying it on the outer chair with his hat on top. He positioned himself comfortably on the bench and lifted his briefcase to the table, opening it and removing his iPad and the small bundle of post before returning his briefcase to the floor. He carefully positioned the iPad in its closed case at right angles to the edge of the table, with the neatly squared pile of post alongside. He put a hand on each knee, took a deep breath and briefly closed his eyes.

For a moment his mind returned to the train. The clash of the mugs became the clatter of the carriage and he felt his body sway slightly as if he was continuing the trip to London. He wondered if his fellow travellers had ever remarked to themselves that he didn't complete the journey any more. Probably not, he decided. Would he ever have noticed if they had been the ones to change their destination?

It had been six months since it happened. After all the restructurings at work, he supposed it was inevitable that he couldn't dodge the bullet any longer. Even so, the announcement had come as a shock. Charles-the-CFO had done his best; Gerald could acknowledge that now. He'd honoured Gerald's long service and loyalty by giving him the news before the rest of the team, but there was nothing he could do to alter the outcome. All their work was being relocated to an offshore Centre of Excellence, meaning Gerald's own excellence was now peripheral. Redundant.

For a while he'd deluded himself that he could change the organisation's mind. He'd worked even harder on preparing his department's work for its new home, thinking that this would buy him a place in the new regime. He remembered word-for-word how Charles had burst that bubble. Gerald had gone to him clutching the letter that had just come from the Human Resources team, which had confirmed the date of his last day with the company. Charles had listened to his stuttered questions and sighed. "Gerald, I'm sorry if you've been under any misapprehension. I thought it was clear. I really appreciate all the work you've done with the offshore team, and I realise that they may not be perfect yet, but there are plans in place to allow for a bit of a bumpy ride for the first few months until it all gets bedded down. I'm really very grateful for all the work you've done, but there's no change in the overall decision. Your position is redundant, and that date in that letter is your last day with the company. There's no changing it."

Gerald had seen in Charles's face that this was final. He had turned and grasped the door handle in nerveless fingers, and remembered

Charles's parting comment. "It's really not all bad, Gerald. I've seen the figures you were given. Your pension is healthy, and the package is generous. I'm sure you'll see it that way eventually. It's not really redundancy for you – it's retirement."

Gerald brought his mind back to the present and opened his eyes to see a cup of steaming filter coffee on the table. Beryl must have brought it while he was in his reverie. He looked round and she waved to him from the counter, calling, "I'll open your tab, don't worry. You're tired this morning. Late night?"

Gerald smiled ruefully in acknowledgement and lifted the tiny jug of milk. He slowly spiralled a stream into the cup, stirred the mixture and found his mind returning magnetically to that day.

He had managed until then to keep it all from Beth. He'd reasoned there was no need to worry her with speculation, but after that conversation with Charles, Gerald knew that she would have to be told. She had long since stopped asking after his day at the office. On the evenings that she wasn't at book club, movie club or her pottery class, she chatted over dinner about the antics of Gorgeous George, their grandson. He wasn't often asked to contribute, he realised, so he'd have to seize an opportune moment. It came as she passed him the gravy boat.

"There's a presentation at work this week about early retirement, thought I'd go along," he'd offered as he poured. He hadn't yet said the word 'redundant' out loud and its softer cousin sounded less threatening.

"Retirement?" Beth had echoed in astonishment. "Why would you want to do that?"

Gerald had placed the gravy boat carefully on its saucer. "It's not such a strange idea, surely?" he'd asked. "I have to stop working sometime."

"Well, yes, I suppose so," Beth had answered. "It's just I've never heard you mention anything like it before! Are you sure you're ready to retire? Wouldn't you get bored?"

"I thought that we could spend more time together," Gerald had offered. He'd looked across the table at her but her gaze remained fixed on her plate, where she was cutting chicken into tiny chunks. After a pause, Gerald had continued, "And I could take up new hobbies . . . the doctor said I should try golf. It would help my back."

"Oh yes, golf!" Beth had exclaimed in what appeared to be relief. "Yes, I suppose there's golf. That's a good hobby. And there are other ways you could fill your day. I saw some courses on at the community centre. There was clock-fixing, you'd like that. And of course our garden always needs sorting out. But can we afford to get along without your salary?"

"I'd get a pension," George had said slightly huffily. "Still, it was just a thought. Are there any more potatoes?"

They hadn't spoken of it again. Beth had never asked how the 'presentation' had gone and Gerald had let the subject drop. He couldn't help but notice that the time-filling exercises Beth had proposed were all solitary. His decades of long hours had let Beth build an independent life and she clearly didn't picture the two of them as strolling into their sunset years hand-in-hand.

As his last day with Baxter Ellis had approached, Gerald noticed that more and more people were congratulating him on his retirement, while commiserating with the rest of the team on their redundancy. His years of seniority seemed to set him apart. "Wish someone would hand me a retirement package like Gerald's got," he had heard one of his team saying to another by the coffee machine.

But everyone had missed the point. Gerald hadn't wanted to retire. Gerald wasn't ready.

So he hadn't.

On the first morning after his last day at Baxter Ellis, Gerald had woken before the alarm as normal. He had dressed, brought Beth her cup of tea in bed and kissed her goodbye before walking to the station. His plan had been worked out in advance; there was no point in investing in a full season ticket anymore. So on Mondays, he'd go ten stops; Tuesdays, nine; Wednesdays, eight until he was six stops away on Fridays. He had decided that that should be far enough to make it unlikely to run into anyone he knew.

Gerald told himself that it was all about giving structure to his day. He had quickly developed a pattern in his five new 'offices', as he thought of the stops on his weekly journeys. It turned out that in these places, which previously had been only names he passed on his commute, there were plenty of activities to fill the time. With agnostic enthusiasm he joined Catholic coffee mornings, Quaker discussion groups and a beginners' Arabic class at the mosque. Wearing the trainers he concealed in his briefcase each evening, he walked the unfamiliar streets like a tourist. He attended lunchtime recitals and a 'Know Your iPad' library course. There were never any questions; most people, Gerald found, accept you at face value if that's all you offer them.

He didn't even really think of it as deceiving Beth. He didn't exactly lie; he simply didn't volunteer the information that his daily routine had altered. Charles had been right about the pension; combined with his redundancy payment, there was enough and they did not have to adjust their standard of living. They had always lived within their means in any case.

The summer passed quickly. Beth commented that he seemed to have a new lease of life. "You're getting a bit of colour in your cheeks. You must be coming out of that office occasionally at lunchtime. Well done!" she had volunteered one evening. "Is Charles finally letting up on the workload?"

Gerald shook himself and lifted his coffee mug to his lips. He was getting nowhere with this wallowing in the past. He opened his iPad's cover and logged on to the café's WiFi, then navigated to his morning's task. As the page loaded, Gerald glanced around at the patrons who had joined him and angled his screen to ensure it wasn't reflected in any of the wall mirrors.

He briskly tapped in his password. This was a good time to start with his colleagues in the States. Late in their night, it was sometimes easier to catch them off guard, or to join a meeting already in progress as participants dropped offline. Soon he was immersed in the brisk exchange, concentrating on reading his opponents' minds through the flickering images they placed on the screen.

It was some time later that Gerald slowly became aware that someone was standing near his table. He tapped once more on the screen and raised his head, wincing as a pain stabbed across his shoulders. His eyes watered as he shifted his focus from the small screen to the woman who stood beside his table with a questioning look on her face. She took pity on his blank expression: "Don't worry, you were miles away. I just wondered if you wanted a refill? It's free," she explained.

Gerald coughed, his throat was dry. "Yes, please," he rasped.

The woman poured black coffee from a percolator jug. "It's Darren's latest bright idea," she confided. "He wants us to be more like *Friends*, you know, the TV show? In their coffee shop, the server wanders round giving refills. 'We're not New York!' I told him, but did he listen? Anyway it only applies to filter coffee, and hardly anybody who comes in here orders that. But I thought of you straight away, and I knew someone would use it on Tuesdays at least. See the poster?"

The coffee slopped dangerously in the jug as she gestured toward a nearby poster that said 'Free Refills!' in bright letters above a photo of a steaming mug. "Thing is, you can't tell from the photo what's in the mug, can you? You have to read the small print. Some woman shouted at me last week, called it false advertising. 'I just work here,' I told her. The attitude you get from some people is amazing. Still, can't knock it . . . A job's a job, right?" She twitched a final smile at him and walked away.

Gerald felt his answering smile grow sardonic with his gaze fixed on her retreating back. His hand dropped away from the iPad and down to his side. He felt automatically for the loose piece of braid on the edge of the seat cushion, grasped it gently between his thumb and forefinger and rubbed. The fabric was much smoother than when the piece had first become loose, several months ago.

He remembered how his umbrella had caught on the seat cushion as he slid it under the chair, pulling the braid away with a sharp, snapping sound. He'd stared at it in dismay, and glanced around to see if anyone had noticed. No-one was looking, so Gerald had taken the seat and spent the next hour subtly pushing the loose fabric back inside the ripped seam. Since then, this had been his favourite seat.

It had been around that time that he'd started exploring the internet as well. Fresh from his course at the local library, he'd noticed the posters in the coffee shop offering free WiFi and decided to try out his new skills. It had taken several weeks, but soon he was navigating sites like a pro and found that the wettest summer on record was pleasurably whiled away in meeting like-minded people in the virtual world, chatting in online fora about any of his interests from cricket to calligraphy.

It was a throwaway comment in one of these chat-rooms that had sent him in a new direction. Someone mentioned that they'd doubled their stake in a bet on the weekend's rugby, and named the site they'd used. Gerald thought he'd have a look. Until now his only experience of gambling had been an annual trip to William Hill to place the family's bets on the Grand National. When he'd walked in to those shops, with their bare floors and newspaper-covered walls, he'd felt like a new cowboy in town in a Western saloon. The room had seemed to hush as he entered, as the regular gamblers registered his strangeness and dismissed him as being of any threat.

The online counterparts were different. The colourful websites beckoned him in and were surprisingly easy to use. He simply had to input his credit card details and then his betting selections were just a tap of a button. Always a rugby union follower, Gerald found it added an extra frisson to watching the games if he had a stake in the outcome. Then one rainy day, an accidental swipe of the screen had dropped him onto a page where he could play some games himself. He hadn't played poker since university, when he and his friends would meet weekly for a late night session over whisky, cigars and stakes of pennies. Still Gerald found that the thrill was the same even when the beverage was coffee and the time was day.

Gerald's phone shrilled in his top pocket and brought his focus back to the present. It was Beth, he saw. "Hello, love . . . Woke up OK then? . . . No, no problems on the train . . . Yes, it is a bit noisy here, I've just popped out for a coffee. Sorry? A tub of crème fraiche, yes of course, I'll pick that up on the way home. See you later . . . No, I won't be late back. Bye . . . Bye."

Gerald's eyes fell on the pile of post he'd placed on the table that morning. He lifted the top envelope and pulled open the stubborn gummed edge with a finger. He pulled out a thick bundle of closely typed paper and his eyes fell immediately on a bold figure on the first page. Surely it was a misprint? He leaned forward and feverishly thumbed through the remaining pages. There were eighteen of them in all, with line after line of transactions all showing the same vendor: BetZonline.com.

Gerald looked anxiously around the coffee shop as if waiting for the hidden camera to appear. He laid the sheaf of papers on his iPad and closed its cover over them. Shaking, he shoved the table away and stood abruptly. He picked up the iPad and walked over to the toilets.

Behind the door, he laid the iPad on top of the wastepaper basket and turned to grasp the edge of the basin. His eyes traced his features in the mirror. There was no outward sign of what he was feeling. The same bland, calm face as always looked back at him. He turned on the cold tap and plunged both wrists under the stream, carefully turned the tap off fully and shook his hands over the sink. Taking a deep breath, he turned around and picked up the iPad. He sat on the closed toilet lid and opened the iPad's cover. The figure jumped out at him again. He hadn't been seeing things.

They'd never had a credit card bill that large, not even when they had splurged on the anniversary cruise. There was page after page of transactions with the betting site. Bets placed on national games and on his own, starting small but quickly escalating. There were hundreds of them, and this was only the last month's expenditure. Gerald shuddered to think what he'd already spent since that statement had been printed.

A knock on the door brought him to his feet. Clutching the iPad, he opened the door and staggered past a little girl who was hurrying towards the ladies' loo with a woman. He returned to his table and poured milk into the cooling cup of coffee with a shaking hand. He tore open a packet of sugar and poured it in before adding another, his eyes gazing straight ahead.

There was only one thing for it. He'd have to be more strategic with his bets: bet bigger, but play fewer games. He could win it back. Beth never needed to know. Gerald steeled himself and opened the iPad again, quickly logging in to his preferred site. He just had to find the right people to play with.

Gerald lost count of the number of free refills he drank that day. He barely lifted his eyes from his screen, intently concentrating on the next round of cards. The corner of the credit card bill peeked out from under the iPad like a baleful fairy. Gerald played on.

He played like a man possessed; swapping between tabs on his iPad to maintain simultaneous games of poker and backgammon. Finally, noticing that the battery icon for his iPad was glowing red, Gerald leaned back from both his virtual and his actual table and closed his eyes. It was no good: he couldn't do enough to claw back those numbers. He reached out for his coffee and found it had gone cold.

There was no escape. He'd have to tell Beth how he had been spending his time for the last six months and how today meant that they would have no income for at least the next six.

This wasn't what either of them had signed up for. He wasn't sure whether it was worse to be the architect of your own downfall or the victim of someone else's mistakes. No doubt Beth would let him know.

Gerald slowly rose and pulled back his shoulders. He lifted his briefcase and tucked the iPad and the accusing sheaf of papers inside. Carefully he lifted his raincoat and slipped it on, neatly tying the belt, and left the coffee shop. Nine stops till his confession. He supposed that it would be a relief not to be alone any more.

INSTANT COFFEE

by Phil Tysoe

DARREN hurriedly picked up a jar of instant coffee from behind the counter with one hand as he slipped his mobile back into his jacket pocket with the other.

"Beryl, I need to pop out, it's a family thing," he said. "Please tell the others, but I shouldn't be long and Elizaveta can lock up if needs be. She knows what to do." Opening the coffee shop door, he called over his shoulder, "I've got to run!" and, without waiting for a reply, rushed out into the street.

When he got to the care home, his father had insisted on returning to his room just as he always did. Darren started after him, intending to follow him out of the communal lounge, all mismatched high-backed chairs clustered together into small groups on a nondescript brown carpet, but a hand on his arm stopped him. "Thank you for coming so quickly. I know you always do, Mr Samuels. It's just that it's happening more often now."

Darren met the carer's gaze and started to reply. "Yes, I know Miss... er... Mrs...." He trailed off realizing with a certain irony that he temporarily couldn't recall her name, lost somewhere amid the rush from the phone call requesting he come and the dash round the corner from the coffee shop to the home.

"Mrs Stanway. Call me Heather, Mr Samuels. We're not so formal here."

"Of course. Heather. I'm so sorry. Must be this place!" The instant he said it he regretted it, and Heather's sudden flush betrayed a mixture of annoyance and hurt in response.

"We try our best, Mr Samuels. Our very best. I appreciate it can be difficult but – "

"Heather, I'm sorry," Darren interrupted. "Really, I'm sorry. It was a stupid joke and I didn't mean anything by it. I've just run from work and I wasn't thinking. Really, I think everyone does a wonderful job here and I know how difficult Dad can be."

Heather gently took hold of Darren's elbow, her other hand lightly pressed against his shoulder, as if to direct him towards the corridor down which his father had now disappeared. Darren almost said something about being able to manage perfectly well on his own but stopped himself: he didn't want to offend her again and, besides, in truth he *wasn't* managing perfectly well on his own.

"Let's catch up with your Dad," said Heather, "before he gets any more upset."

Darren felt the grip on his elbow tighten and the hand on his shoulder subtly apply enough force to cajole him to move, and he let himself be guided towards his father's room.

"Perhaps you ought to go in first," suggested Heather when they reached the door. Darren nodded.

"We should be okay for a bit. I'll call you if we need anything."

"Of course, Mr Samuels. I'll just be in the lounge."

Darren watched her walk back up the corridor before turning to the door of his father's room. As always, for fear of further disturbing him, he knocked lightly before opening it.

"That you, Mary?"

"No Dad, it's me," replied Darren.

"Thought it was your Mum," he muttered. "Should have known better. She never comes anymore."

Darren thought about trying to explain it all to him again: *She can't come Dad. We lost her, she died eight years ago. You know all this Dad, you know it all but you keep forgetting.* Instead he looked back at his father's face, at the scowl that masked his confusion and sadness, and did what he'd been doing more and more frequently of late: he lied. "She's running the shop, Dad. Come on now, we talked about this. If I'm here one of us has to stay behind and keep the place open."

His father grunted. "Shop? What are you talking about Darren?

161

What shop?"

"The coffee shop, Dad. Our coffee shop. The one me and Mum opened up just by the High Street."

"Your Mum doesn't like coffee shops, Darren. What's she doing opening one of those? Waste of money she always says. Why'd you want to pay all that money for a cup of something you can get a full jar of for the same price?"

"She doesn't drink it though, does she Dad? She sells it to people with me. We're a good little team, me and Mum. She's good with the customers and I look after the money, sort out the stock, things like that."

Sustaining the lie was easy now: it was sprinkled with enough truth that Darren slipped seamlessly into it. He didn't own the shop but he did look after the money. He had to: every penny he took home in wages was keeping his father in this place.

"Well, as you're here you might as well make yourself useful. Seeing as you're in the business, make us a cup of coffee will you Darren?"

Darren nodded. He picked up the coffee jar and a couple of mugs that his father kept in the room and went down the corridor to the communal kitchen. He weighed the kettle in his hand: it felt full, so he switched it on before opening the jar and dunking a teaspoon into it. It was an indulgence really, he thought, bringing his own coffee but it was the brand they'd drunk as a family and his father didn't really like the catering stuff the care home provided. The kettle boiled and he poured the steaming water over the granules. 'Making coffee,' he thought distractedly. 'That's all my life is now, making coffee.' Sometimes, back in the shop, he liked to imagine each of the cups he made as a moment, a memory he could attach to whichever customer he was serving. Here was Gerald with his iPad and filter coffee. Here's Arnold having his usual cappuccino. Then he imagined freeze-drying each of those memories, reducing the essence of each cup down and capturing them somehow in his instant coffee jar, his to release for his father every time he brought them to life with hot water. If he could help him retain something, just hold onto his daily stories of the customers in the shop, then perhaps it might all come back. He liked to imagine that one day he'd get just the perfect mix of coffee and water and milk that would unlock all of the memories, the ones he had stored there in the jar and the ones that had been lost. On that day his father would taste the drink, look up at him with a smile, and say *It's alright now, son. It's alright. I remember it all, Darren. I remember it all and it's all going to be alright.*

He returned to his father's room, placing the mugs and the jar on the table between their chairs. He took a quick glance at his father as he sipped his drink but nothing in his eyes changed, there was no moment of magic. As usual they sat in silence for a few minutes, each with little new to say to the other until, eventually, his father asked him what he'd been up to lately. Darren had long run out of things to tell him: his life was completely wrapped up in running the coffee shop and visiting the home. That was all he had. He'd taken to filling the empty space between them with stories, as if to thaw one of those imaginary freeze-dried coffee granules and release the moment it contained. He told his father about the people he saw in the shop, sometimes the real things they told him and sometimes wild flights of fancy, imagining what they might get up to in their lives. He gave them families and friends and hopes and dreams. He presented it all to his father, their lives wrapped up with his, as his family, friends, hopes and dreams. He knew that each time he spun the stories they would be forgotten and that he could tell them afresh the next time he visited.

"I've got to get back, Dad," Darren said, suddenly noticing the time. "I shouldn't leave Elizaveta to lock up."

"Elizaveta?" His father's eyes narrowed in suspicion.

"Mum. I can't leave Mum to lock up," corrected Darren, but it was too late.

"Who's Elizaveta?" His father was agitated now, gripping the arms of his chair and leaning forward. "Who is she? Why are you lying to me?"

Suddenly his father stood up, shaking with rage, and grabbed at the jar of coffee on the table in front of him, knocking it to the floor.

"Who are you? What are you doing in my room?"

Darren hadn't fully screwed the lid back on to the jar and coffee spilled out onto the carpet, thousands of tiny dark fragments lost across the brown fabric as his father called out for help. Frantically Darren took to his hands and knees, picking up small piles of the granules and replacing them in their container as best he could. It was no good though, too much had gone. He looked at the jar in his hands, now only a quarter full, and began to cry.

The door burst open and Heather's hand on his shoulder finally stopped him.

"Steady now, steady now, Mr Samuels. It's not worth getting upset. It's only coffee after all."

HAZELNUT
STEAMER
by Debbie Hunter

THE last hour of the day always seemed the longest. Beryl didn't need to look at the clock: her back and feet told her it was nearly time to go home and she wondered if they would hold out until closing time.

She regretted persuading Maria to leave half an hour early. "Don't worry," she'd told her. "I'll lock up. You go off and have a bit of time at home. Darren need never know – and we're not likely to have a rush this late in the day . . . I'll manage," she added sensing Maria's uncertainty.

At the time the look of gratitude on Maria's face seemed worth the ache in Beryl's feet but now she couldn't wait to turn that key and go home, especially since the coffee shop was empty. It seemed to exude an air of sulky gloominess when devoid of customers, not helped by the darkening autumn evening.

Even the man who sat all day looking at his computer had gone, with a face as miserable as sin – he hadn't even left a tip, despite Beryl pointing out to him earlier that it was 'Free Refill Tuesday'. He was a bit of a grump, hadn't even heard of *Friends* – who hasn't heard of *Friends*? He always came into the coffee shop on Tuesdays, smartly dressed, carrying his newspaper and computer. Beryl had watched him tapping away for hours on end, covering the screen whenever she came near him. He had puzzled her for weeks until finally she had concluded that he was a spy.

Maybe she could leave a bit early, but it would be just her luck for Darren to come back. She didn't want to get on the wrong side of

Darren. He was a nice enough young chap – she'd worked for worse managers – but she knew that if he was given the chance to replace her with someone younger he wouldn't hesitate for long before giving her the push. And 'the push' she did not want. There were times when she thought she might have to look around for a second job. But could her aching bones handle more work?

Money was tight and luxuries were becoming fewer and fewer. She used to have a regular flutter on the horses but had stopped that a few months ago. She still did the Lottery – she would have to be really skint before she gave up the excitement of that. 'Got to be in it to win it,' was her motto. She patted the pocket where she kept her Lottery slip. She knew her numbers by heart.

And, besides that, she'd worked at the coffee shop for years, long before Darren came on the scene. She even thought of some of the regulars as family, although she kept that to herself. She worried about them as if they were her own brood. She had a child to worry about, but he was so far away that her concern couldn't reach him.

Taking a cloth out of her pocket, she sighed as she started to wipe one of the mirrors. She took great pride in keeping them sparkling even though they were becoming the bane of her life, never clear of sticky finger marks. But she loved her 'little kiddies' who came into the coffee shop, even the mischievous ones. Beryl never considered them naughty; to her there was no such thing as a naughty child – only an incompetent mother.

She dabbed at a small handprint, about the size of a four-year-old she supposed. Justin was four – the little grandson she had never seen, never held as a baby, never played with, never wiped his finger prints off a mirror . . .

She took another cloth and applied it vigorously to the chrome coffee machine, perversely using the ache in her back as a spur to a spotless gleam. The only spots on this machine would be the ones on young Darren's reflected face as he inspected Beryl's workmanship. The latest in coffee-producing technology was Darren's pride and joy and he only allowed Maria and Elizaveta to use it as they were 'trained baristas'. She wasn't trusted with operating such an elaborate machine; according to Darren her advanced age only allowed her to clean mirrors and wipe tables – and only at the busiest times to take the odd tray or extra order to customers. Not that she minded. She didn't even like coffee much, preferring tea or milky drinks like Ovaltine or Horlicks, but who drank those these days? They certainly didn't feature on Darren's modern menu alongside 'mochas' and 'steamers'.

Beryl wondered what a steamer tasted like. She'd seen Maria making one earlier in the day, deferentially adding hazelnut syrup to the frothy milky foam, the same foam which topped a cappuccino. Beryl was amazed how much Darren charged for a cup of froth but Maria told her that the flavoured syrup was especially imported from some exotic location and was very expensive. "Eet come from China or somewhere – or maybe Eetaly . . . I don' know but eet cost a lot. Darren buys this fancy stuff but 'ee pays us . . . 'ow you Inglish say . . . peanuts?" Maria's shoulders had shrugged in disdain; she didn't care much for Darren's tight-fistedness particularly where salaries were involved.

Beryl's aching back longed for a sit-down and a comforting milky drink. Oh, what the hell! She placed a mug of milk under the sparkling chrome tap and twiddled the long handle just as she'd seen Maria do. Nothing difficult about that. The steam and swoosh of the liquid was curiously satisfying. The sleek glistening bottle of the foreign hazelnut syrup lured her from its elevated position on the top shelf. Cautiously she reached up and, with trembling hands, poured a few drops of the precious liquid into the foamy milk. She thought of looking at the bottle to see where the syrup came from but that would mean getting her glasses out of her pocket and she couldn't be bothered with that.

A lone muffin left on the counter radiated an 'Eat Me' message, making Beryl feel like an elderly Alice-in-Wonderland. She was tempted – she knew the muffin would be delicious. Antonia had yet to make anything which, in Beryl's opinion, was not mouth-wateringly sumptuous. Beryl was very fond of the girl and admired her baking skills. Taking on Antonia had been one of Darren's better ideas. Beryl thought of her as a girl 'in need', a complex young woman with 'issues'. Beryl would have liked to have solved Antonia's issues for her, putting her arm around the young woman's shoulders with a motherly "Tell me what's troubling you, love – a problem shared is a problem halved." But Antonia, always kind and polite, never gave Beryl that maternal opportunity or satisfaction. Beryl reached out to take the muffin, then thought better of it – drinking the steamer was enough of a risk.

She took the drink to a table and glanced at a newspaper lying there, open at the travel page. She noticed a picture of a gigantic red rock encircled by a magnificent sunset – 'Australia in all its glory' she read. Australia, halfway round the world, where her son lived with his Australian wife and Beryl's unseen four-year-old grandson Justin.

She took a cautious sip of the hazelnut steamer, careful not to scald her mouth. It could have done with a bit more flavour she thought but she didn't want to chance her luck. Darren might notice the lowering level in the syrup bottle and get suspicious. Despite spending a fortune on those exotic liquids Darren could be very watchful of costs and made sure everything was accounted for. Beryl wondered how he managed to keep cool when customers broke cups but even though he was inexperienced and had miserly ways he did have a knack with the customers, always the professional and courteous manager.

She remembered clearing up a broken cup that day. Who'd broken it? Oh yes, a smart woman of about fifty, white as a sheet she'd been. Beryl was quite concerned at the time but she'd noticed that the woman had been laughing with her friend as she left, so she must have got over whatever had upset her.

Beryl leant back in the chair and put her feet up on the table, her hands and mind comforted by the warmth of the mug held against her chest. A hot drink was just what the doctor ordered. Beryl couldn't imagine a cold drink giving off the same comfort. She thought of the poor old lady who'd come in today, the one in the wheelchair whose son had bought her the Freddolatte. At least Beryl assumed it was her son and the women were, probably, her daughters. Sour old lot, that family looked. The old lady certainly hadn't thought much of her cold Freddolatte. Perhaps her son had ordered it for her on purpose just to be spiteful. Mind you, Beryl agreed with the old lady. All that freezing drink nonsense was another of Darren's fads.

That lovely chap Arnold had been in the coffee shop again today. He'd let slip that it was his birthday. If she'd known she would have given him a card. 'Dear Arnold,' she imagined writing, 'Many Happy Returns of the Day. Love Beryl'. 'Love' would make him squirm with embarrassment and he would be taken aback that she knew his name. How did he think he could come into the coffee shop three times a week yet no-one would know it? It was written plainly for all to see on his glasses case along with his phone number. Beryl noticed these things.

'Most people are lovely,' Beryl thought, although you sometimes got the odd one who was trouble. Like that aggressive woman who'd accused her of misleading advertising with the Free Refills. As if it was Beryl's fault. She'd quite thought the woman would never come back but surprisingly she was there today. Beryl never forgot a face, especially one on such a brittle bitchy character. It was almost a pity that the woman hadn't started her complaining nonsense again today; Beryl would have enjoyed seeing how Darren coped with it.

On the whole, she reflected, most of the people who came into the coffee shop were good-hearted folk. She wouldn't really want to leave here and the thought of finding another job was frightening. She sipped the steamer. Despite needing a touch more flavour it was rather pleasant, pity it was so pricey.

She reckoned it was about time to pack up and go home, Darren wouldn't be making any late surprise visits now. Might as well take the newspaper home with her, perhaps she could have a go at the crossword. She leafed through the pages to see if the paper had one, preferably not too highbrow.

As she folded the paper at the games and puzzle page her eye caught sight of a row of numbers. She read them. She took a slip of paper out of her pocket and read them again. A sceptical voice in her mind cautioned her not to believe her eyes. She fumbled for her glasses, noticing how her hands had started to shake. She read the numbers again.

Such a shame no-one was around to hear her whoop of pure delight, to witness the zeal with which she tore out the Australia advert from the newspaper, and to see the look of satisfaction as she added a triple shot of hazelnut syrup to the remains of her steamer.

BIOGRAPHIES OF THE AUTHORS

Lesley Close was born in Oxford in 1956 and went to school in Buckingham. She is the youngest of three children and the mother of one. A voracious reader from an early age, Lesley somehow managed to avoid virtually all of the English-language literary classics until middle age! Her favourite writers include Ruth Rendell, Phillip Pullman, William Trevor and Alice Munro among (many) others. Lesley learned tap dancing and singing as an adult, and is a keen cyclist, walker and photographer. She has two non-fiction books in print and her third title, an e-publication, hit the 'shelves' in May 2013.

Linda Cohen was born in Leicestershire over 200 years ago. An only child, she was educated (sort of) in Highgate. Linda left school early due to a crisis in the family, and eventually found someone in the City who took pity on her and offered her a job as secretary. She spent the rest of her years regretting her lack of schooling. Always a lover of creative writing, just before leaving school she won the *Cadbury's Writing Competition* for all schools (which is her only claim to fame). Married with two children, and five grandchildren, she was inspired by her eldest grandchild (who was in the middle of 'A' levels at the time) to 'carry on learning – even now'! At a very young age she was inspired by the Brontë sisters, and now reads everything and anything. Linda worked as an estate agent for many years before having a complete career change: she trained as a social work assistant and worked on the spinal injuries unit of The Royal National Orthopaedic Hospital until she retired.

Emma Dark has lived in Amersham for the past twenty years. She is married with two grown up daughters. Emma joined the writing class a few months ago after this set of stories started to grow and has found the help and support of her fellow students a great inspiration to get some words down on paper. She is currently working on her first novel.

A native of Sussex, **Angela Haward** is an in-comer of twenty-five years standing in Amersham. She is married with three adult children and, having retired from her day job in 2014, she is reinventing herself in her original incarnation as a writer. After university, she worked as an industrial journalist, but the advent of children put paid to this for several years although she did a bit of freelance work. She has had a few articles published and has also produced a French-language teaching aid for primary school children which is still available on Amazon. In between, she has done a lot of other things: she has worked in school business management, carried out PR work for a charity, set up and run a second-hand children's clothes shop (with other activities) as a service to local mothers, travelled, looked after old people – it goes on. Since joining Sally Norton's *Just Write* class eighteen months ago, Angela has been inspired by the rest of the group and has found the joint exercise of producing the Coffee Shop stories a stimulating revelation in co-operation. The group has raised her faltering ambition into second gear. Let's do another one!

Richard Hopgood was born in 1952 in South East London, the son of a policeman and a nurse and one of five children. After boarding school in Sussex he studied English at Oxford and London. His childhood ambition was to be a naturalist and a poet, neither of which transpired. His favourite short story writer is John McGahern.

Debbie Hunter was born and bred in Berkshire. At the tender age of sixteen she emigrated with her family to South Africa where she lived for thirty years. Although nostalgic for the heartbeat of Africa she now considers herself extremely fortunate to be living in Bucks where she enjoys the beautiful countryside. She also appreciates the close proximity to London, where her passion for all things royal and historical can be accommodated.

Liz Losty was born in Belfast and graduated with a degree in Politics from Queens University, Belfast. Liz travelled after graduating, before settling in London and pursuing the well-worn path to a career in the City. She now lives in Buckinghamshire with her husband, three children and two guinea pigs.

Originally from Canada, **Christine Payne** studied English Literature and Psychology at university and came to England to "get into publishing". This manifested itself as becoming an internal communications manager in the healthcare industry. A lifelong Anglophile, Chris found that her early viewing of *Blackadder* and *Monty Python* on CBC (Canadian Broadcasting Corporation) allowed her to slip seamlessly into British culture. She has lived in Amersham for twenty years with her British husband, with whom she has three children.

Now that she has retired from careers as diverse as a freelance musician and an officer in the Royal Naval Reserve, **Vicky Trelinska** has the time to concentrate on writing. Originally from Sussex she was educated at St Swithun's School, Winchester, and trained as a pianist at the Royal Academy of Music, London. So far her writing successes include an article published in *Yours* magazine, a story short listed in a *Writers' News* competition and letters and press releases printed in local papers. She is married to a retired GP and has a step-son.

Faced with a mid-life crisis, **Phil Tysoe** couldn't carry off a pony tail and didn't have the money for a Porsche so he decided to rekindle his early life love of writing instead. By day he works in the field of retail consumer insights and by night he watches too many *HBO* box sets, listens to a lot of Bruce Springsteen, and plays the guitar. Badly. He lives with his wife and daughter in Amersham.

DEDICATION

Dedicated to The Royal Marsden Hospital, for the wonderful work they do.

In support of

About The Royal Marsden Cancer Charity

Every year The Royal Marsden provides treatment and care for more than 50,000 cancer patients and is at the forefront of cancer research. Its work influences how all cancer patients are treated and cared for, not just in its own hospitals but all over the world.

With the help of The Royal Marsden Cancer Charity, The Royal Marsden can continue to push the boundaries and benefit cancer patients, wherever they are.

The Royal Marsden Cancer Charity raises money to help The Royal Marsden provide world-class diagnosis, treatment and care for cancer patients, and supports the hospital's pioneering work in cancer research.

By supporting The Royal Marsden in this way the charity aims to make life better for people with cancer everywhere and strive for a future without it.